KANE 5

King Coopa J

KANE 5

Copyright © January 2024 by King Coopa J

1 – KING & QUEEN

"You have to hide," Jar said, his eyes focused on the vehicle parked in front of the cabin. "Your sister is home."

"Noti's home," Aayla hurried over to the window and spotted the vehicle. "I thought she wouldn't return from visiting our mother until tomorrow."

"I guess not," Jar turned to Aayla and held her back from the window. "I'll get her in the shower, and that will give me enough time to drive you back to Zuwarah."

"Ok," Aayla put her hands on Jar's face and gently caressed his cheeks. "Promise you'll tell her that we want to be together?"

"I will," he kissed her as he heard footsteps on the porch. "Hurry through the back."

Things could have taken a nasty turn if Noti had discovered them. Everything had to go according to plan, especially with Aayla. She was the key to unlocking his future, and a fallout with Noti would not work in his favor. The cards were dealt, and the only thing left was to

1

play the hand, for better or worse. Aayla's actions would determine the outcome.

Jar hurried to the driver's side after helping Aalya into the vehicle. He shut the door and started the motor. He didn't want it to seem like he was in a hurry. Noti was home and he told her he would travel to Zuwarah to meet the General. That's how it had to feel with Aayla as well. One sister knew the truth, and the other did not. Aayla could betray him. The General was indeed infatuated with her. And Noti could leave him. To him, blood is thicker than water. In any case, looking out for himself and controlling the weapons trade was more important. He had to make sacrifices under all circumstances.

"Do you think she's aware of us," Aayla asked, still facing the window.

"She didn't say anything," Jar responded. "I would not have made it to the car." He looked at Aayla and smiled. She was absolutely beautiful and the key to his success. The General and his men were out drinking at a bar. Jar, Noti, and Aayla happened to be at the same establishment celebrating their new partnership, which moved them to Africa. Things could not have gone better after arriving in the country and meeting the General in the first week. The General approached Aayla, and from there, it was history.

"If my mother finds out," Aayla turned her head towards the front windshield. It was dark outside, but she could see a reasonable distance. It was her first time leaving Jamaica, and she wanted to take in the beautiful scenery. She had several things on her mind. However, the top priority was closing the deal with the General. Doing so would indeed make the queen happy. She now had an opportunity to tell her mother how she felt about Jar, hoping she would approve. On the other hand, Noti would be a problem she would have to deal with later.

Jar interrupted Aayla while keeping his attention on the road. "There won't be a problem with your mother. My father is gone, and I'm in charge of the operation. We closed the deal with the General because of you. Our future is bright."

"And Noti," she whispered. Her older sister would be hurt. There was a concern about how things would play out when the conversation arose. Jar would soon have to tell Noti the truth. Eventually, Noti would confront her about sneaking behind her back to be with him.

"We can tell her together if that would make it easier for you," Jar turned right onto a dirt road that stretched for an hour, heading toward Zuwarah. He took this route at least five times a week. Either to visit Aayla or the General in Tripoli.

Aayla kept her eyes out the window, trying to comprehend how she would feel if the shoe was on the other foot. She came close to deciding not to tell Noti anything about their relationship.

Jar took his eyes off the road for a split second to glance at Aayla. He noticed that she didn't respond. He put his hand on her chin, turned her head his way, and smiled playfully. "There is nothing we can not do together besides name our children."

Aayla's face got brighter. Jar's comment made her smile. "You don't like Kane and Abel?"

"Those are names from the Bible," Jar said. "We should give them Jamaican names like Jevaun or Damerae."

"Your choice of names will kill our boys," Aayla said evenly. "The General knows who we are. He saw our faces. We are Jamaicans on African soil, trying to establish a smuggling business. People will come for us . . . our friends, family." She shrugged. "We must protect our boys by giving them different names, a life in America far from this environment."

Aayla's perspective opened his mind to the possible dangers ahead and life. He hadn't put any thought into it until now. The smuggling business could ruin his family. Anyone linked to him could die for his mistake. His competitors and enemies could be hostile. If war found them in the United States, his children should carry non-Jamaican names. Jar faced Aayla. "You thought about this?"

"I have," Aayla said while looking into his eyes.

Jar smiled at her. "Those names may grow on me."

2 – ABEL

"Ah . . .," I groaned, lying on my back in the middle of the road. I had attacked Kane, and he got the best of me. My face was in pain, and my body felt paralyzed. I couldn't hear anything. It was utterly silent. I tried to open my eyes, but they had swelled shut. Kane had used my face as a punching bag. I should have finished him in the first fight. He was more powerful than before, as though he used all his time to train. I let my anger get the best of me and approached the situation wrong. It was over for me. I had nothing left to give. All of the strength in my body was gone.

I felt dirty, beat up, and on the edge of death. The sun in this part of the world didn't make it any better. Libya was not the place where I wanted to die. The heat was absorbing the small fraction of energy I had left. I thought about praying, which put a smile on my face that hurt like hell. It lasted less than a second before the pain kicked in. My life drastically changed after I took Jar's life. You don't honestly see yourself until it's your turn to face the reaper.

I coughed twice and felt the blood leave my mouth and land on my cheeks. My fingers began to twitch, and there was a tingling feeling in my toes. I regained movement in my hands and feet. The numbness in my arms and legs passed, and they were functional. My mind told me to get up, and my body said no. "Come on," I encouraged myself to move and mustered the strength to turn over onto my stomach.

"Look at what we have here," I suddenly heard someone speak out angrily. I recognized the voice but couldn't put a face on it. The person sounded older and had an American accent. Not African, which told me the man followed either Kane or myself from Atlanta.

"You couldn't pick a better time to show your ugly face," I heard Kane's voice not too far from me. His mind was off of killing me, was my first thought.

"Where is your bitch of a mother," the familiar voice asked. I was in no condition to answer anyone, but what had happened earlier crossed my mind. The General captured Gina, my aunt, and my mother right before I attacked Kane.

"Fuck you," Kane growled. Whomever the man was, they weren't on good terms by the way they spoke to one other. Their altercation alleviated the answer that the person had followed me to Africa.

While Kane focused on the man, I took the opportunity to crawl away. I spotted the Jeeps we arrived in parked before the first building leading toward the warehouses. My vision was still a bit blurry, so I couldn't pinpoint which vehicle I'd traveled in. The closest truck was my only option if I wished to survive.

"Oh, you're a tough guy," he said, and I stopped. I ceased movement to avoid alerting them of my intention to escape. "I'm sure he'll tell me." There was a short pause. "Goodbye, smartass."

In the back of my mind, a little voice said he was speaking to me. I held the position until I heard another familiar voice come from a woman. "Don't you dare," Kim, I thought. I'm the last person she would save. "I'll fuck up your whole day."

"Please, you're not that dumb," The man was speaking the Kim. "You'll kill us all, you stupid bitc—"

A loud explosion erupted that seemed to shake the earth. My body was still intact. I'm alive, I thought before receiving a jolt of new energy. I moved with hast toward the Jeep. Every inch along the way lit my bones on fire. I made it to the vehicle without dying and reached for the door handle. It opened, and I put my arm on the sidestep to pull myself from the ground.

"You stupid bitch!" To my surprise, the man was alive—*Bang, bang, bang.* I heard gunshots. "You fuckin' stupid bitch!"

I was almost inside the Jeep when a negative thought hit me. What if the keys are not in the ignition? I didn't have the strength or the time to search the other vehicles. I shut the door and hoped the sound didn't draw attention.

"My face," the man shouted as I checked for the key. "Ah . . . you bitch!"

Fuck! The key wasn't in the ignition. I checked on top of the dashboard. Nothing. I had to lower my head to the center console just to see clearly. My vision was no longer blurry, but the swelling didn't go anywhere. I couldn't have been any happier when I saw it. I put the key in the ignition and started the motor. I should've been gone, but Snake and Bam came to mind.

I could have returned to the warehouse to see if they were alive. Kane was back there with his crew. Snake and Bam could be dead. I had to make a tough decision because I still needed them. The rebels were strong but not bright. I didn't get a response on the transmitter, and the compass on the watch was still green. If they were alive, the indicator would have been red and led me to their location.

The love of my life and Aayla needed my help. The General took the only road heading away from the area. I couldn't tell you where he took them. The road stretched for hours. There were a few dirt off-roads, probably leading to active regions like this one run by rebels or the General's men. I couldn't save them without the rebels, not in this condition and proper planning. He would've murdered them on the spot. Instead, he took them hostage. Whatever the case, they were significant to him.

I reluctantly decided to leave both parties. Snake and Bam were sacrifices for my cause. I couldn't save them, weak and alone. Kane

8

already did a number on me. The General spared Gina, Aayla, and my mother. I still had time to regroup with the rebels and save them.

Bang, bang, bang! "Get the fuck outta the truck!"

The gunshots interrupted my thoughts. I looked in the rearview mirror and saw someone standing behind the Jeep. The mirror was dusty, making it hard to see the figure. I didn't realize how difficult it was to breathe until that point. My chest panted, taking in deep breaths as if I had sprinted to the vehicle. Slowly, I eased the clutch into reverse. I could see the barrel of the weapon through the rearview. That, I could make out without a problem.

"I said get out of the fuckin' veh—"

I floored the pedal, and the Jeep sped out in reverse. Gunfire erupted, and I figured those were desperation shots. I missed the person and immediately put the truck in drive. What, I thought. The person who stood in front of the vehicle was Jordan. If I hadn't noticed him standing by the plane. I wouldn't have been able to confirm it was him. Half of Jordan's face was destroyed. It didn't matter. I pressed the pedal to the floor, heading in his direction. The lunatic stood there, fired, and missed every shot. I stuck him with the vehicle. Jordan rolled up the hood and smacked the windshield. It shattered but stayed in place. I couldn't see where I was driving and ended up swerving off-road. I couldn't shake him. After riding over a few dips and bumps, he slid off the hood and latched onto the passenger side door. Lucky sonovabitch, I thought.

9

I drove wildly, trying to throw Jordan from the vehicle. I glanced at him. He had his arm inside the door and managed to open it.

"I'm gonna . . .," I hit a bump in the road, and Jordan bounced around and nearly fell off the truck. "Fucking . . . kill you." He tried to raise the weapon toward me, but another bump threw off his aim.

I swerved the truck all over the road, keeping the crooked agent off balance. Jordan had a wild look in his eyes as he fought to maintain a grip on the vehicle. Clouds of dust filled the air at every turn. It was thick enough to somewhat block my vision. I had to conjure the strength in my arms to control the Jeep. Driving off-road made it difficult by stiffing the steering wheel. It felt like the power steering shut off for a brief moment.

I drove over a ditch that caused the Jeep to dip and shoot upward toward the sky. Let's say the shocks on the truck's front end worked wonderfully. I could have won first prize in a hydraulic contest. The truck bounced three times and then rocked back and forth like a seesaw. There was no way Jordan could hang on after that rough ride. Then I heard a growl that verified he was still hanging onto the vehicle.

"You . . . stupid fuckin' kid," he struggled to get the words out.

I didn't bother to look at Jordan. I focused on the road ahead, straightening the truck toward a smoother path. Suddenly, a sharp pain manifested in my ribs. Everyone felt broken. The situation worsened when Jordan grabbed my arm and threw off the Jeep. The dust cleared,

10

but it didn't help much with my driving. Jordan was crazier than I initially thought. He was after Kane, and now he wants me. Jordan, the white cop, my mother, and an assassin came together. Kane and his crew were also in Africa. They came for Jar's safe. How did they find this location and the time I would come? Oyoo was the only person who knew.

Jordan tugged my arm hard. "I said stop the fucking truck!"

I glanced at him and got a clear shot of his face. Something horrible happened to him. It looked like someone dipped one side of his face in acid. He couldn't have been in great shape, but he felt strong as an ox. He jerked my arm, pulling me downward in the passenger's seat. The dashboard blocked my view and I couldn't see the road anymore. My eyes were on him. The gun fell onto the floorboard. The only way he could grab it was to let go of my arm. My foot remained down on the pedal as I drove blindly. I grunted, trying to muscle upward to see what was in front of me. Jordan was almost inside the vehicle. His legs were still hanging out of the door. I thought they would have broken after driving off-road. Apparently, they were working fine.

Jordan made it inside the Jeep, and I struggled to keep him off me. I'm a much stronger man than him, but my wounds made us equal in strength. I saw him reach for the weapon. It was imperative to stop him even though I would lose complete control of the steering wheel. I needed my other hand, so I let go. The truck moved freely as if the power steering reactivated, maneuvering the vehicle from side to side.

11

Our hands locked on the gun. I held the barrel, and his grip was around the handle. He couldn't shoot because my large hand allowed me to get a finger behind the trigger, preventing the gun from firing. However, that didn't matter after a few seconds of battling with Jordan. We both were in trouble.

The truck headed in the direction of a building. The same destroyed structure we passed on the way to the warehouse. Another decision I had to make. Jordan, the gun, or controlling the truck. None were great options, and all would kill me. Jordan and I fought inside the Jeep. He was entirely in the passenger's seat. I kept my hand on the gun, and the other locked around his left wrist. As the truck approached the building, I figured this would be my end. I took my foot off the gas and tried to find the brake pedal. I couldn't keep pressure on it because I was consistently thrown around in the seat. I managed to apply a bit of pressure before the truck collided with the wall. Pain shot through my body as I released Jordan and the weapon. I couldn't tell if I had died because everything immediately went dark.

3 – KANE

I sat in my father's chair at the warehouse, contemplating our current situation. The diamond rested in front of me on the desk. I've been through a lot in the past twenty-four hours. Abel was in Africa. I left him in a bloody mess on the roadway with The Planner. Who knows, Jordan could have murdered him by now? The General captured my mother, Rick, and two other women. I don't think he'll kill them yet. He needs them for something, possibly for the rock. Another problem presented itself. How long could I stay in the warehouse before Abel, Jordan, or the General decided to stop by? I could prepare for an ambush or simply leave with my crew.

I had several things in my favor. The nerdy kids are a part of Abel's crew. Something inside me said he left them for dead, considering he didn't know the taller one had the diamond. He could backtrack for it. Doo-Rag told the General's lieutenant that we had the diamond, and I'm sure he wanted it. I tried to trade it for our safety, and the plan got ruined. The General brought an army, and I didn't. He would have killed us after finalizing the deal. That would have been an easy decision for him. We don't compare to trained soldiers who kill for a living. Doo-Rag's crew was made up of young boys, barely teenagers. I got this far with them, but that's about it. I wouldn't think about challenging an army with them.

My thoughts were interrupted when Kim, Smoke, and Doo-Rag walked into the office. Kim approached first, walked around the desk, and put a hand on my shoulder. Smoke and Doo-Rag stood before us, waiting for me to speak. They were relying on me for a plan. My crew followed me to Africa to help find my mother. They're already rich thanks to the deal between Jordan and the General. The money I found in the Humvee solidified our future. They didn't have to come, but they did, putting their lives in danger for me.

"What's on your mind, dawg," Smoke broke the silence. "How you feelin'?"

I thought long and hard about an answer before he asked the question. It was on my mind when I was sitting here alone. "I think you, Bear, Bruce, and Kim should go home."

"What," Smoke's face turned sour. "Hell nah, you're trippin', my guy."

"No way," Kim looked into my eyes, and I knew what she was about to say was serious. "I'm not leaving you here alone. You must be out of your mind. The General . . . Abel, rebels . . . any one of them could kill you if you're caught. I'm not taking that risk, so forget about it. I'm staying."

"Kim," I said sincerely.

"Don't start," she interrupted without taking her eyes off me.

"Sis is right," Smoke spoke up. "We started this shit together, and that's how we'll finish. I'll do anything for mom dukes."

I sighed.

"I don't know why you suggested that we leave you," Smoke continued. "After what happened to you, your father, mom, and . . .," he looked at Kim. It was a touchy subject regarding what happened to her. It was something we all felt.

"It's alright, Smoke," Kim spoke up.

Smoke lowered his head. "I promise I won't ever let that go. Abel will pay for that, sis. On everything I love."

"Thank you, Smoke," Kim said sincerely. "That means a lot to me."

My family was here until the end. Even if it doesn't end well. Redd is dead, and I don't think I can go through someone else close dying on me. Mentally, it's too much to handle. It was already enough stress, praying that nothing would happen to them.

"Kane," Doo-Rag listened to our conversation without saying a word. He took off his shades before finally speaking. "I suggest, for now, keep your family close. The General will guard all exits until he gets what he wants, or you all are dead. Sending them away now could mean death. The soldiers at the airport work for the army, and the hotel employees are also the General's eyes and ears. There is nowhere to hide. He will find us eventually."

15

"What would you suggest we do," I asked Doo-Rag. "You know the land better than any of us."

"Stick to the plan," Doo-Rag said. "Kill the General."

"Listen, dawg," Smoke turned Doo-Rag's way. "Dat shit won't work. We're wanted, and the General knows wassup with us. Bruh about to be on high alert. Fuck him. Let's find Mom Dukes. Get her the hell out and dip. Simple."

"I wish it were that easy, Smoke," I said, thinking of other options.

"Ok, so what do we have to our advantage," Kim threw out there for anyone to answer.

"Shit . . . the diamond maybe, guns," Smoke said with a shrug. "Nah, dem niggas have guns too. Fuck."

"That's it," Kim said with new life in her voice.

"What," Smoke replied. "The diamond?"

"No," Kim answered. "Not the diamond."

"Sis," Smoke said with sarcasm. "The rocket launcher won't be enough. We only have one anyway."

"I'm not referring to the rocket launcher," she told him.

"Then what," Smoke asked.

"Doo-Rag," Kim looked at him. "Do you know where the General keeps hostages?"

"There are camps all over Libya for prisoners," he answered. "They could be anywhere."

"What about high-value hostages," she seemed eager to express her plan.

Doo-Rag thought about it for a second. "A soldier assassinated a prominent public figure in Nigeria. The capture of his killer was essential. The General found this man and took him hostage. No one knew where the man was held, and one day he escaped. This happened a long time ago."

"Ok," I said sarcastically. Doo-Rag's story about the soldier wouldn't help if he didn't know where the man was kept. I turned to Kim. "What are you getting at?"

"What if we knew the location of your mother," she began. "We could hack the building's security system. Take control of the cameras. And, if we knew the layout, sneak inside and save your mother. The General's army won't be in the same place. He's on high alert, right? So, his men will be throughout campsites, airports, hotels, etcetera. They won't be as strong, and I don't think he would expect a security attack."

"Sis, buggin'," Smoke spoke up. "No one here is like that. Maybe Jimmy Tang, but he's in Atlanta."

"That's where you are wrong," Kim said with confidence.

"Who are you talking about," I asked.

"The kids in the other room came with Abel," Kim said. "And they don't look like hired muscle."

"Do you actually think they'll help us," Smoke asked with his eyebrows raised.

"They don't have a choice," Kim told him. "I'm sure Bear and Bruce can convince them to cooperate."

Smoke shrugged for approval.

"You want to get the kids to help hack the security system," I began. "Then sneak inside and save my mother. We still have to consider how many soldiers will be on-site even if we know the floorplan, which we don't have."

"I know someone who may know the location of the assassin," Doo-Rag told us.

"What will it cost," I asked. That was more important than anything. I was running short and needed to re-up on some cash.

"A favor," Doo-Rag put on his shades and crossed his arms.

"What kind of favor," I asked.

"We'll have to see when we get there," he said. "This man is trustworthy."

"That's good to know," I said. "Where can we find this man."

Doo-Rag smiled. "Get your things ready. We set out in two hours."

"Where are we headed," I asked, perplexed.

"To visit Oyoo."

4 – RICK

"What is the deal with you," Rick asked. It's been a few hours since he had food or water. The holding cell wasn't that bad. He saw worse conditions throughout his law enforcement career. He had to figure out how to get his mind off his stomach.

Aayla sat back on the bunk in her cell. She let out a sigh of frustration. The white man brought in with her had been complaining since they arrived. She tried ignoring him, and that didn't work. She could only do one thing since they were being held together in the same block. She decided to speak. "Why do you complain, white man? You can spend your time working on an escape plan?"

"Is that what you're doing over there," Rick asked. He put his hands around the cell bars and looked at Aayla. She didn't appear fazed by being in a holding cell, possibly waiting to die. "And by the way. My name is not, white man. It's Rick."

Aayla smirked and sat up. "What do you want to talk about, Rick?" She sighed. "Food, water? Maybe you want to talk about how they will torture us before cutting off our heads?"

"Jeez," Rick was shocked by Aayla's blunt response. "Lighten up. I just wanna talk to you. I wasn't aware Mrs. Simmons had a sister until a run-in at a rebel post. They thought she was you."

"She would not speak of me to anyone," Aayla got off the bunk and walked over to the cell bars. What the white man said intrigued her. She glanced at Rick. She could smell fear on him and see it in his eyes. Men like him don't get out alive in situations like this one. The General would get the information needed and then kill him. "Don't waste your time on her. She doesn't care for anyone and will betray you."

"She doesn't appear untrustworthy," Rick couldn't match Aayla's stare, so he looked away. He knew nothing about her, but he could tell she had been through a lot. Her physical features were very different from Mrs. Simmons'. Her arms and legs looked powerful. The relentlessness in her eyes garnered respect. He could tell by her static posture that she could be domineering toward men. "Did she betray you?"

"Look at me when I speak to you," Aayla asked. "How can I trust someone who doesn't give me attention? Looking away is a sign of weakness. The men you will have to deal with know this."

Rick was surprised by Aayla's response. He felt her presence in the room even if his eyes weren't on her. However, she did have a point. Jordan, Adrian, Abel, the rebels, and the General seemed cut from the same cloth. He had to be better and gain the confidence needed to survive. He raised his head and made eye contact with her before speaking. "Did she betray you?"

"Yes," she answered, keeping her eyes on him.

"Tell me what happened," he asked with confidence.

"Tell me what happened at the camp with the rebels," Aayla smiled, thinking about how her older sister pretended to be her. When Aayla was a young girl, she would follow in Noti's footsteps pretending to be her. She found it amusing now that Noti was following in her footsteps.

Rick thought back to when the rebels captured him. He thought they would kill him for sure until Mrs. Simmons saved his life, along with Jordan and Adrian's.

There was still time left to find them. Rick had to turn into someone else. Someone more savage. That was the only way to survive in Africa. The FBI agent was gone for now. He would have to sacrifice Jordan and Adrian in return for his life. They would do the same to him. Rick decided right then he had to become the hunter, and the brothers would be his first meal.

5 – ABEL

What happened, I thought. I couldn't remember anything as I slowly regained consciousness. Every bone in my body ached. My ribs felt ten times worse than before, and so did my legs and arms. I blinked several times to get a clear view of my surroundings. After a few seconds, my vision was no longer blurry. I was lying on the outside of a wrecked Jeep. Suddenly, I heard two voices speaking near me.

"What happened to your face," an unfamiliar voice rang out. "Did someone throw acid on you?"

"It was the fuckin' kid's girlfriend," the second voice was very familiar.

I couldn't see the position of the men, but they were close. I tried to roll over on my side, but the pain was too great. I slowly regained a bit of strength while lying helpless on a dusty road. The destroyed Jeep was a dead giveaway that I had been in an accident.

"You let a girl do that to your face," the man sounded amused by his response.

"She had a fuckin' rocket launcher," he got upset.

The man began to laugh.

"You're a fuckin' idiot," I recognized the man with the familiar voice speak up. "You let a girl do that to your face." He mocked the guy. "Obviously, it was the same bitch who shot down the plan."

They got closer, and I could see them hovering over me. I couldn't move if I wanted to, so I didn't, hoping they thought I was still asleep. They hadn't noticed me, so I closed my eyes and began to think about how I got into this situation. I tried to recall what had happened. The only thing that came to mind was the wrecked Jeep. Was I driving, I thought. Who are the men? Where am I?

"Yeah, about that," he said after calming down.

"Did you recover the gold," the man asked. I heard his voice on my left side.

"I accomplished finding and loading the gold in less time than we did as a group," the man to my right answered. "I stashed it inside an abandoned building just outside of town."

"Fuckin' genius," the man on the left was sarcastic about it.

"Why do you care," right-side answered. "It belongs to me now. Don't renege on our deal?"

Gold, I thought. Not only did that play on my mind, but a girl shot down a plan. Either I was making a movie, or this was a dream. I knew nothing about the gold or the girl with a rocket launcher. What did I get into? I peeked just to catch a glimpse of the men. The man on the right had on all-black, and the man on the left was dressed in army fatigued. They had good size and appeared dangerous.

"You just hold up your end of the deal," left side spoke up. "Help find the boy, his fuckin' girlfriend, and the mother. I want them dead." He growled.

The man was serious. I could hear it in his voice. He wanted people to die. Women, at that. I couldn't figure out why I was here and what I had to do with them. Nothing came back to me. I also had to consider I was scared for my life. I focused on the men instead of trying to remember how I got here.

"Wait a minute," the man with the unfamiliar voice said with a sense of urgency. "There you go changing our agreement once again. You're never true to your words, big brother. You didn't say anything about finding the kid and his girlfriend. Just the woman, Noti. And that's what you and I agreed to."

"I know what we agreed to, little brother," he snarled. "Need I remind you? Feel free to cancel. I'll take my half and do the job myself. I mean . . . what's easier than killing three people for five million in solid gold bars? Jobs like that don't fall out of the sky. You know what I mean?"

The man on the right side must have reluctantly agreed because he didn't say a word after a long moment of silence.

"That's what I thought," the man on the left responded. "It's always a pleasure doing business with you, little brother."

24

"Call me little brother again, and I'll slit your throat," I didn't expect that to come from the mouth of the man on the right.

The man on the left laughed. It sounded wicked. The guy had to be a nut job. Something was off about him. I didn't have a good feeling about either of them. I could tell they were professionals by the way threatening words rolled off their tongs so easily. They spoke about millions of dollars in gold bars and killing people as if it were an everyday thing. The man on the right said jobs like that don't fall out of the sky. I wondered if I was part of a job. Did I do something wrong, and someone hired them to kill me?

"Awe . . .," the man with the evil laugh replied with sarcasm. "Did I hurt your little feelings?" he joked. "Take off your panties and put on some boxers. You're acting like a cute little girl who thinks she's tough. Put your pride to the side and help me with this sonovabitch. Would ya?"

"Why do we need him," the voice came from my right side. "He's dead weight. You should kill him or let him go."

My heart began to race. He suggested killing me to the man I thought was crazy. I wanted to get up and run even though I didn't know if they had guns. However, sitting here was the same as waiting to die.

"He's Noti's son," he answered. "We can use him. Also, find out what he knows. Think about it. He's here in Africa at the same place and time as us. That's not a coincidence."

"I don't think about anything but who I have to kill," the man on the right side answered.

"I forgot you have a one-track mind," I heard the man on the left chuckle. "Don't overwhelm yourself using your brain. Grab his legs and help get him in the truck."

"You know," the voice came from my right side. "I could have taken the gold and left you on your own."

I heard a sigh come from the left side. "Just grab his legs."

I got some troubling information from the man on my left. My mother was in danger and for some reason . . . I came to Africa. I heard the man on my right move toward my legs. They intended to put me in the back of a truck. They couldn't possibly be referring to the wrecked Jeep. It didn't look driveable to me. The man who led the conversation needed me to find my mother so he could kill her. I got that part. I was still unaware of who was the other kid and his girlfriend. There was a connection between the men, us, and five million in gold bars.

"On the count of three," the man on my left sounded above my head.

"On three," the man by my feet confirmed the count.

"One," the voice came from above.

"Two . . .," said the man by my feet.

I felt a sudden cloud of dust kick up from the ground and enter my nose. I couldn't control the tingle inside my nostrils. The man grabbed my ankles and prepared to lift. I felt the man above place his hands under my arms. I couldn't pretend to be asleep any longer and I sneezed hard on the guy.

"What the fuck," the man by my head shouted and let go of my arms.

My body jerked in reaction to the sneeze, causing the man to release my ankles. I swiftly got on my feet. My first intention was to run. I noticed I was much larger than the man before me. The man I had sneezed on covered his face with his hands. I quickly turned to the other man and wrapped my hands around his waist. I tried to slam him to the ground, but he reversed the move and pushed me out of the way. I stumbled forward and nearly fell to the ground.

"Fuckin' gross," I heard a voice of frustration come from behind me.

I took off after regaining my balance. I didn't have to think about it. Every stride I took got harder. I felt my entire body in pain. I couldn't remember a time in my life when I felt worse. From the bottom of my feet up to my face was an irritating numbness.

Bang, bang, bang!

I stopped suddenly. I didn't feel any bullet wounds after hearing gunshots. I panicked while checking over my body. My adrenaline was pumping. I'm aware when your heart rate is that high. It's difficult to know if you are hurt without actually seeing a wound.

"You see," I heard from behind. "He's a smart kid."

27

I took a deep breath and decided to turn around. The men stood next to each other as if they enjoyed watching me act hysterical. The man holding the gun had damaged the right side of his face. The wound looked fresh, and he didn't seem bothered by it. The guy in all black had a smirk on his face. I felt like it was a joke to him.

"You missed," the man in black said.

"He stopped. Didn't he," he casually tucked the weapon in his waistband.

The man in black shrugged. "Whatever works for you."

If I was going to die. I wanted to know why. "What do you want from me?"

"Can you believe the audacity of this shithead," the man with the destroyed face turned to his partner. He focused on me after the other guy answered with a shrug. "The sonovabitch next to me thinks I reneged on our deal, but you're the one who reneged on our deal."

My eyes flicked between the two men as I searched for an answer. "What are you talking about? I don't know you."

"Oh please," he waved me off. "You can stop with the shenanigans. You know what you owe me from the museum job. I know you took it from your goddamn brother!" He burst out angrily. I could see the fire in his eyes. He quickly went from zero to sixty.

I tried to comprehend what the man was referring to. Apparently, he was upset about a museum job I had nothing to do with. "You must

28

have mistaken me for someone else. I'm still unaware of what it is you're talking about."

The man smiled. "You can put down your hands and slow down your breathing. You look scared to death, and it's messing with your fuckin' memory!" The man snapped.

"It seems to me you're the one who needs to breathe easy," the man in black responded. "The kid says he doesn't know, so just kill him so we can move on. We're wasting valuable time."

"Let me fuckin' handle this, Adrian," the man growled, keeping his eyes on me. He closed his eyes, took a deep breath, and exhaled. "Ok. I'm gonna ask you one more time. Abel. Please tell me where I can find the African Black Diamond? The really fuckin' big rock I hired you to steal, which you and your fuckin' idiot friends failed at. You wouldn't be in Africa without it."

What the man said blew my mind. I could pretend I knew what he was speaking about and prolong the situation as long as I could until I escaped. That was an option, but his temper could get in the way. There was something he said that intrigued me that I needed to address. I was right all along. "Listen, I understand why you're upset. You're missing something that belongs to you. But . . . I hate to inform you that you've mistaken me for someone else. I'm not Abel."

6 – KANE

"Bring in the hostages," I told Smoke.

Smoke went to the door and shouted into the warehouse. "Yo, bring in the nerdy kids!"

Seconds later, Bear and Big Bruce escorted the kids from Abel's crew into the office. They stood in front of the desk with worried looks on their faces. I didn't take my eyes off them as I stood from the chair and walked casually around the desk. I crossed my arms and let out an exhausted sigh. I propped back against the desk while facing them. Neither of them held eye contact with me. Their eyes focused on the boots they were wearing. They looked out of place. We all did. Who would have predicted any of us would be in Africa?

I examined the taller kid before speaking. He was frail as if he hadn't eaten in weeks. He reminded me of a kid sent to the principal's office waiting for punishment. We've all been there a time or two. I know I have. His knees were shaking uncontrollably. I wondered if he had shit himself. I'm not the guy who bullies weaker kids. My parents didn't raise me to be that way. However, these two caused trouble for me by helping Abel. I'm not supposed to take it easy with them.

"Are you okay," I asked the taller kid. "It looks like you're about to cry."

"No . . . no, sir," he replied, keeping his eyes facing the floor.

"Don't worry," I said. "I'm not gonna kill you if that's what you're wondering."

"Thank . . . thank you, sir," he stammered as I noticed his hands ball into fists.

"You hear this nigga," Smoke scrunched his face. "Thank . . . thank you, sir. Ya hoe ass over here about to have a heart attack."

Bear and Bruce laughed at Smoke's comments. I thought it was funny as well, but I kept my cool.

"Chill out, Smoke," Kim eyed him.

"Damn . . . you throwing my government out there for these niggas," Smoke shot back at Kim.

"That's not your government name, fool," Kim shook her head.

" . . ." Smoke began to speak but took a second to think about it. "You're ri . . . ght."

"Nigga what you smokin'," Bear asked.

"Aye . . .," Smoke was cheesing hard. I could see all of his front teeth.

"I get it," I said, getting back on task. "Your parents taught you how to behave. I know a well-mannered person when I see one. But you don't have to call me sir."

"Yes . . . yes, sir," he said and glanced at me before looking back at his boots.

"This nigga," Smoke erupted. "Yes . . . yes, sir. What he say? You didn't hear my dawg, pussy."

"Smoke," Kim looked at him again. "One more time."

"My bad, sis," Smoke apologized and backed away. "These fools work with Abel, and you know how I feel about it." He pounded a closed fist in the other hand. "Imma step before I slid on these niggas."

"Thank you," Kim acknowledged him.

I could mentally grasp how Smoke felt about them. They were a helping hand that contributed to what we went through. They had shot at us multiple times, broke into Kim's apartment to steal the diamond, and above the rest, helped kidnap her, which was devastating to us all. Smoke's anger represented how ninety-nine percent of us would act under the same circumstances. I couldn't blame him.

"He's gone," Kim told the taller kid. "You have nothing to worry about."

The kid nodded without saying a word. He glanced at her and looked away. Smoke was out of the room, and the kid still looked terrified. "She's right. You're good."

The kid looked at me and then at Bear.

"He's scared of the big guy," the smaller kid poked his chest out, trying to appear manly.

"The big guy, huh," I said and looked at the taller kid. "Is that right? You're scared of my boy?"

"He . . . he's a monster," he replied. "Keep . . . him away from me. I was out cold for . . . for three days after he knocked me out. The longest I ever slept was . . . was twenty-one hours, forty-six minutes, and thirteen seconds after drinking a half-bottle of NyQuil. My mother was pissed I missed school that day."

"Bruh," Bear looked at Big Bruce and chuckled.

"You knocked out the skinny kid, dawg," Bruce looked at Bear. "And I thought I was a bully."

"He got active," Bear threw his hands up. "You feel me."

"Oh," Bruce had a look of acceptance on his face. "In that case. It's up."

"He gave him two black eyes and a broken nose," the smaller kid sounded angry.

"You straight, playboy," I stood up and fixed my posture. "You're looking at me as if you wanna do something. We can throw hands if you want. One-on-one. Considering everything you helped Abel put us through, I'm trying to be nice."

His chest deflated real quick. "I . . . don't want to fight. Look at us. You physically outmatch me. You are only treating me this way because of my size. Just say what you want from us."

33

I smirked and stepped closer to the kid. "Your name is Bam, right? I remember the girl . . . what was her name?"

"Gina," Bear spoke up.

"Gina. That's right," I continued. "That's what she called you the night we got in a squabble. Well then . . . Bam. You see the tough guy behind you?" I waited for him to acknowledge Bruce. "We had a disagreement in prison and fought. Size doesn't matter to me. I'll whoop you if you're ten feet tall."

Bam tried to maintain eye contact to show he wasn't afraid. A tear rolled down his cheek after a second.

I wiped the tear from his face with my thumb. "Or we can be allies and get through this together." I brought my hand down on his shoulder hard enough to make his knees buckle.

Bam got his knees together and looked up at me. "I . . . like the last option."

I nodded, backed away, and leaned against the desk, taking the same position as before. "This is my offer. I need you to hack into a security system. Do that, and you can go free with the diamond."

"Wait a minute," Kim raised a finger. "You're gonna let them go with the diamond?"

"We don't need it," I shrugged. "I just want to get my mother back safely. That's it, and we can go home."

Kim slowly shook her head as though she was unsure I was making the right decision. "If you say so."

"Any of you have a problem with me giving up the diamond," I asked the crew.

Bear was the first to answer. "Mom Duke is more important. Plus, I wanna go home anyway. Nigga sleepy."

"I'm good wit it," Bruce spoke up.

"I have your friendship, son of Jar," Doo-Rag said. "I got what I wanted."

"Smoke," I shouted so he could hear me.

"Fuck it," Smoke shouted without showing himself.

I knew he was listening to our conversation outside the doorway. My guy was always on point. "We're all good then." I turned my attention back to the two nerdy kids. "Do we have a deal?"

"You'll kill us after completion," Bam's eyes wandered between Kim, Doo-Rag, and me.

"As a man," I held out my hand. "I give you my word. No harm will come to you or your friend."

Bam looked down at my hand, and for a minute, he hesitated to shake it. "Deal."

"I can't," the taller kid cried. "Abel has been good to me."

"I didn't expect that," Kim whispered loud enough for me to hear.

I gave the taller kid my attention. "And you're the one she called Snake. You know . . . I saw yearbook pictures of you, Gina, Ali, and Abel. You guys have to be best friends. It's fucked up because that's likely what brought you here in the first place. I know it's hard, but let

35

us know where you stand. You guys are smart and were living the dream at Yale University. Look at you now, fuck around and get diced up by a rebel in dirty sandals. Shit real out here, and I know you wanna go home. My friend Redd died because of me. I think about him every single day. I wish we had stayed home that day. All I'm saying is make the right decision . . . for both of you."

"Um . . .," Bam held up his index finger. "I attended Harvard."

I looked at him as if to say, shut the fuck up.

"I attended Harvard," Bruce joked in a proper tone. "Would you prefer the caviar, my good man?"

Bear chuckled. "Nigga, you a fool."

Kim gave them a look that said stop playing, and they fell back in line.

"What about Abel," Snake asked worriedly. "It will ruin our friendship if he finds out I helped you."

"I'll take care of Abel," I assured him. "We have some . . . family issues to get straight."

Snake lowered his head and began to speak. "Abel helped me when no one would. I didn't have any friends at school, and he became the first. We planned to do great things together before all this happened. You're right. I am here because of our friendship. It's not about money for me. I view the world through a different lens when it comes to life. However, my life is on the line. If I don't accept your offer. I'll die. You won't convince me otherwise. I know what Abel did to you."

36

Snake looked at Kim. "I'm sorry for what happened. His actions could seal my fate. If I do agree . . . then . . . who am I? Friends don't betray each other's trust. With that being said . . . I'll help if it will free us and . . . you can keep the diamond."

"And I didn't expect that either," Kim muttered.

"Are you sure about that," I asked.

"That thing has been nothing but trouble since we got it," Snake glanced at Bam and then at me. "The rebels will think we're trying to escape with it and kill us. It's too dangerous. She won't let us out of the country with it."

"She who," I asked, confused.

"The woman pretending to be Abel's aunt," I could hear the seriousness in Snake's voice. "Queen Aayla. She knows we have it. And get this . . . she named Abel their new leader."

7 – I LOVE YOUR SON

Noti sat across from Gina in an isolated room where no one could hear their conversation. She left Rick behind because the girl was more valuable to her. Although, she did feel sorry for how things turned out for the American FBI agent. Capturing what her husband poured his blood, sweat, and tears into was priority number one. Nothing could get in the way of the mission. Jar told her there would be casualties at war. Mr. Chase was just another do-gooder trying too hard to make a difference.

"What is your name, girl," Noti asked evenly. The girl had to be trouble by involving herself with Abel. Noti looked the girl over. She was young and pretty, two traits that drive men crazy. There was an aura around the girl that felt dangerous.

"What does it matter," Gina said with attitude. She rolled her eyes. "You don't care what happens to me."

Noti smirked. "How do you know for certain? I did free you. At least you can tell me your name?"

"Humph . . .," Gina crossed her arms, looked away, and shook her head. "I'm still here if that's what you call being free."

Gina wouldn't make it easy for Noti. She kept her composure without showing a sign of frustration. "I can open the door if that's what you want. Who knows what the General and his men would think? A pretty girl like you . . . alone in a country where trafficking women is at a high. They could fetch five . . . maybe ten grand for you." She shrugged. "You would think men run the sex trade, but it's women who are untrustworthy."

"Is that who you are," Gina asked. She kept her head turned to the side as she looked at Noti from the corner of her eyes.

Another shrug. "I'm a mother. That's it, nothing more." Noti sighed.

"Abel never mentioned you," Gina told her. "You're not that good of a mother."

Noti smiled. "Abel has always been a unique child. When he did something bad as a young boy, he would run to me in fear of his father. I would hear his little footsteps in the hallway before he made it to me. He would sit on my lap and point at the door, waiting for his father to appear. I wouldn't let anything happen to him. He was safe with his mother, so he wouldn't mention me to anyone but the people he trusts."

"Abel trusts me," Gina was offended by Noti's words. It felt like a knife to her heart. "We've been together for two years."

"What's two years compared to a lifetime," Noti intertwined her fingers and rested her hands on the table. "A girlfriend to a wife or a mother."

"He didn't tell you about me, so what's the difference," Gina thought she had Noti. "And I'm his girlfriend."

"How could he," Noti kept a straight face. "He dropped me off at a mental health facility two years ago. My husband's death weighed heavy on my heart. Did he not mention it?" Noti wanted to see if Gina knew Abel had murdered his father.

Gina looked around the room. Abel hadn't mentioned anything about his parents to her. She only knew he had fallen out with his brother after the museum heist. "No," she answered in a whisper.

Noti could feel she had Gina's attention. "It's traditional in our culture to meet the parents for approval if you love someone. Do you love him?"

"With all of my heart," Gina answered.

"I see myself in you," Noti said sincerely. "I loved Jar the same. We were young, and I left Jamaica with him for Africa long before moving to America. It's ironic because you are doing the same with my son."

Gina didn't say a word. She was lost in thought, thinking why Abel had not mentioned anything about his parents.

Noti kept pressuring her. "Men," she sighed. "Can't live with them . . . can't survive without them." Noti stood. "I'll leave you to yourself

40

since you don't need my help." She turned toward the exit. "The door will be open."

Gina looked up and saw Noti leaving the room. "My name is Gina."

Noti stopped before turning the doorknob. A smile spread across her face. "Gina," she said before facing her. "It's nice to meet you."

8 – ABEL

"You know what," the guy with the scarred face turned to the man in black. "Maybe I should kill him?"

The man he called Adrian shrugged. "Do what you need to do, Jordan, and get this over with. The more time we spend on this guy, the less time we have to find the others. You didn't hire me for this guy, but I'll take care of him for . . . half price since you've been so kind."

Jordan, I thought. I couldn't recall where I heard the name. I held up my hands to let them know I wasn't a threat.

"Stop playing games with me, kid," Jordan looked at me. "Do you want me to kill you for being a smartass?" Jordan tapped the weapon on the side of his head like killers do when trying to comprehend something.

"Of course not," I said honestly, shifting my eyes between them. "I don't know where you can find an African diamond and —"

"The African Black Diamond," Jordan roared. "Fuck! It's not just any fuckin' diamond!"

"Ok, the African Black Diamond," I corrected what I said to please him. "I don't know where it is, and I don't know Abel."

Jordan massaged the left side of his head with the barrel of the gun. "Listen, Abel. You're a smart kid. I don't have to tell you this. You attended Yale University, so stop with the psychological bullshit."

"I didn't go to school at Yale," I responded. "I went to . . .," I paused to think which school I did attend and couldn't figure it out. My memory was gone. I couldn't recall any school I had ever attended throughout my life. "I went to . . .," I tried forcing it out. Nothing. Jordan and Adrian were looking at me, confused.

"Let me guess," Jordan spoke up and took a step towards me. "You can't remember because you think I won't kill you if you pretend to act dumb. And I thought your brother was the idiot. This was the best plan you could come up with. Out of all of the idiots I'd dealt with as an FBI agent, this is by far the dumbest tactic I have ever encountered."

"I have a brother," I mutter, thinking about what Jordan said.

"Yes, numb nuts," Jordan shouted. "Your twin, Kane. The reason my career is over. The sonovabitch."

Kane. My twin? I couldn't help but think if Kane looked like me when I should have been thinking if Jordan was lying about everything. I definitely didn't believe he was an FBI agent. He didn't resemble an officer to me, and his temper was disturbing.

"Go over there and do the thing you do," I heard Jordan tell Adrian.

43

"What thing is that," Adrian responded with sarcasm.

"You know . . . the thing," I could tell Jordan was frustrated. "When you can tell if someone is lying, jackass."

"He's clearly lying," Adrian sighed. "Stop wasting time."

The guy in black could tell if I was lying or not. He's a human lie detector, I thought. There are people in the world who specialize in the department of interrogation. Adrian was one of those people. I came up with a plan that could possibly save my life. "Please . . .," I looked at them seriously. "I want you to interrogate me. If I'm being deceitful, then you can kill me."

Jordan looked at Adrian. "You heard the kid."

"If he's lying," Adrian stepped in my direction. "the price is double." He stopped in front of me. "Hold out your arms."

I did as he asked and held out my arms. Adrian rolled up my sleeves and applied pressure on my wrists with his thumbs. When he did this, I didn't get nervous. As hot as it was in Africa, I didn't sweat one drop. I was eager to find out what was the truth more than anything. I saw Jordan several feet behind Adrian with his weapon aimed at me. He didn't frighten me, assuming he was intrigued by what I had to say.

Adrian locked eyes with me. "What is your name?"

"Ah . . . come on," Jordan snapped. "Ask a real fuckin' question. Where is the diamond, shithead!"

"Shut up," Adrian shouted over his shoulder. "and let me do this."

"Fuck," Jordan through a temper tantrum and spun around several times.

Adrian's eyes were back on me. "What is your name?"

I don't have a reason why I thought about the question. It's one of those things you should know without hesitation. "My name is . . .," I pondered the question. "My name is . . . I don't know."

"Your name is I don't know," I heard Jordan snarl. "That's fuckin' great. He wants to die."

"Do you have a twin brother," Adrian asked.

Jordan said I have a brother named Kane. I wasn't sure if I should say yes, according to what he said, but that would be a lie. I didn't know if I had a brother. "I'm not sure."

"Yes or no," Adrian's thumbs massaged the pulse in my wrists.

"No," I answered, hoping Jordan wouldn't lose his mind. I glanced over at him. His eyes were cold even though I could see the fire in them.

"Alright, last question," Adrian said. "Do you know where we can find the African Black Diamond?"

The question was the easiest to answer. I wasn't sure about my name or if I had a brother, but I did know one thing. "No." I didn't know anything about the African Black Diamond.

"I fuckin' had it," Jordan rushed over and pushed Adrian out of the way, stuck his gun in my face, and fired.

9 – RICK

"Is that what happened," Aayla grinned at Rick. "My men thought she was me?"

"Yes," Rick rested his arms between the bars. "They called her, the Queen."

"The Queen," Aayla hissed. "She wouldn't die for my position." Aayla tried imaging Noti as the leader of the rebel army. Everything she'd worked for came at a cost. Men wouldn't accept her if she didn't shed blood. Aayla killed over fifty men during her rise to the top. Ten, she murdered with her bare hands. She stood out among other women in the army. Her skills would be on display each mission. Even the men praised her and saw her as a competitor to ascend the leadership ladder.

"You don't like that she pretended to be you," Rick observed Aayla. Something was on her mind after he told the story. The sisters had tension between them. His cop instincts spoke to him. Figuring out what happened could give him insight into the feud between them.

"I don't like how easy she became me," Aayla said. "I shed blood on the battlefield. She shed lettuce on a kitchen counter."

"Do you want to live her life," Rick asked. He thought Aayla sounded jealous of Noti. He figured to use it to his advantage to keep her talking. "I know her very well. After her husband's death, I was the detective on the case. Let me tell you, that was my introduction to their family. Their son, Kane . . . put us through hell."

Aayla thought back to when she and Jar first spoke about having boys. Kane and Abel, she named her nephews instead of her sons. She was deeply in love with Jar, and he betrayed her trust. He left her alone in Zuwarah with a broken heart. She painted an image of Jar's face on every life she took until her love for him was gone. Aayla shook the thought of having a family from her mind. "I shaped my life the way I wanted it to be. It seems my sister would rather have my life."

Rick contemplated Aayla's response. She did answer the question truthfully. Noti had changed after their encounter with the rebels. *Queen Noti could be a thing,* he thought. The control she had over the rebels might have gone to her head. At the time, he noted that Noti didn't appear nervous while convincing them she was Aayla. He wondered what had happened to her. Mrs. Simmons' behavior could be related to Jar's death. She had a very noticeable personality change. "Tell me what happened with Mrs. Simmons?"

Rick's words put a grin on Aayla's face. "Mrs. Simmons is the wife of Jar Simmons. I don't know anything about her." She shrugged, looking at Rick's unpleased facial expression. "I can tell you about Noti Wilson."

10 – ABEL

The shot missed my head by an inch. I was lucky to be alive. When I saw Jordan rush over to me, I thought I would die. I dropped down to my knees and covered my ears. The ringing sound inside my head was overwhelmingly loud. What he did only proved I told the truth or pieces of my skull would have been left for the vultures.

The ringing in my eardrums came to a stop. I heard Adrian shout in the background. "He's telling the truth. Stop wasting ammo, dumbass!"

I heard Jordan fire the gun three more times before speaking. "That's why I'm pissed off, Adrian! The accident fucked up his memory. Fuck! I'll never get back the diamond. Sonovabitch, he's useless."

I felt the barrel of Jordan's gun press against the back of my head. "Wait!" I couldn't die after finding out about my family. They could tell me who I am. "I can convince Kane to give you the diamond in exchange for my life. He doesn't know I lost my memory."

Jordan didn't speak. Instead, he applied pressure behind the barrel.

49

I continued, praying he would listen. "I'll steal it if I have to. I need to know what he looks like and where to find him."

"Why would Kane do that for you," Jordan growled. "You fuckin' tried to kill him at the museum, and your baldheaded girlfriend tried to blow up his chick in a hospital while she was in a coma. And that's only half the shit you've done to him in the past two years."

How could anyone be forgiven after putting someone through that much trouble? I couldn't recall any of it. I said the first thing that came to mind because I had a split second to respond. "The same way I convinced you."

"You're gonna tell him you lost your memory," Jordan asked. "That's not a bad idea. Your brother is an idiot."

I felt the pressure of the gun release from my head. I sighed, stood, and brushed off my pants.

"You got yourself a deal," Jordan held out his hand. "The diamond for your life."

Jordan didn't have any intention of keeping me or Kane alive. He had enough of our family, and I could perceive him envisioning a slow and gruesome death for each of us.

I shook hands with a man I didn't trust. The next step was figuring out what led to the accident that caused me to forget who I was. What was I doing in Africa? "Ok, do you have a picture of Kane?"

"Why would I carry a fuckin' picture of a boy," Jordan snarled. He holstered the gun on the side of his waist.

"So you can identify who you're looking for," I said. "That's what officers do when they're hunting for someone."

"Well, I'm not a goddamn officer anymore, smart ass," Jordan got heated faster than an oven.

"He has a picture on the internet," I looked at Adrian after he spoke up. "We can get a connection in one of the nearby towns. And while we're there, I can get some rest. It's been a long day." Adrian got into the driver's seat of another Jeep parked a few yards away from the accident. "Come on!"

I waited for Jordan to move.

"Let's go," he led the way. He opened the passenger's side door. "Get in the front. If you try anything, I'll blow out your fuckin' brains."

It was a meaningful threat to take my life. Jordan meant what he said, and I wasn't about to try him. I got into the front seat. I was so scared that I buckled the seatbelt without realizing it. I wanted to ask Adrian where are we headed, but the look on his face told me not to speak.

"Safety first," Adrian said with sarcasm and started the Jeep.

I gave him a half smile. My face was in pain, and I didn't know why. I touched the side of my jaw, and a sharp pain resonated on the entire right side. "Um," I groaned, pulling away my hand.

"A bandaid will fix that right up," Jordan said like a concerned mother.

"Do you think it will fix your face," Adrian laughed while pulling back the truck.

"Fuck you," Jordan snapped at Adrian. "I like my new look. It's menacing."

"To women," Adrian replied.

We drove for about an hour and a half in silence before I built up the confidence to speak. "What was I doing before the accident?" I didn't look back or say his name. Jordan knew the question was directed toward him.

"Does it matter," Jordan asked evenly. It was the first time I heard him speak without getting angry.

"I need to know why I'm here," I told him. "I want to be aware of my situation if I'm going to help you. Someone could kill me before I get the diamond. If Kane has it and you want it. There could be others."

"I could kill you," he replied.

"Just answer the fucking question," Adrian said out of frustration. "I wanna know myself."

I heard Jordan suck his teeth. "You're here for the same reason I came to Africa. Your father was a prolific weapons smuggler. He has a warehouse at the location we were just at. Your mother guided us to the location. I don't know how you found it or why you showed your ugly face."

"You're being sarcastic, right," Adrian chuckled.

Jordan didn't respond, just sighed before continuing to speak. "Your mother promised me millions in exchange for your brother's life. And of course . . . she betrays me. So excuse me if I get a little murderous. I'm having trouble trusting anyone in your family."

"And the accident," I asked. "Did I do something to you?"

"It's not about you, kid," Jordan answered. "I want your brother and mother. I figured you were my best shot at finding them until you lost your memory. We had a disagreement, and you plowed the fucking Jeep into a building. I lost two hours messing around with you."

"Who am I really," I asked. "Some kind of weapons smuggler like my father? A thief? Did I have the diamond at one point?"

"You're a fuckin' genius," Jordan replied. "That's who you are. My former partner and I dug into your family's history after your father's death. I saw pictures of you that gave me the chills. Not so much now. You're a pussy. After I found out you went to Yale and how smart you are. I figured giving you and Kane a stab at stealing the African Black Diamond. I had no doubt you would get it, but your asshole brother and his friends beat you to the punch. If I had known he'd be a problematic prick. I would've left him out of the deal."

Several things had my mind searching for answers. My father seems to be the key to unlocking my past. His dealings got our family into this situation. He's dead, which wouldn't help anything. I pieced together the information Jordan gave me. I overheard them talking about gold. Apparently, Jordan hired my brother and me to steal the African Black Diamond. Kane was successful, and we went at it with each other for it. We unexpectedly met at my father's warehouse. The location where the deal with down. Something went wrong, and now Jordan wants to kill my family.

Adrian stopped the truck, interrupting my train of thought. "Try not to get lost. This place isn't for tourists. The people here are savage and keep your dick in your pants. The women here are not housewives."

"You don't need to tell him that," Jordan said while opening the back door. "He's a dead man walking."

"I wasn't speaking to him," Adrian shut the driver's side door. "I was talking to you."

I got out of the Jeep and surveyed the town. It didn't appear like the poverty here was similar to the last town. It was night, and half-naked women were moving around freely. Possibly prostitutes. The buildings weren't destroyed but were still in poor condition. The roads throughout the town were paved gravel and not dirt. The choice of travel was bicycles and motorscooters. I spotted three Jeeps like ours. Several soldiers were wearing fatigued pants and shirts. The same uniform as Jordan. I wondered what was their connection with him. They didn't seem bothered by his appearance. They were more focused on the women wandering around in skimpy clothes.

"Follow me," Adrian led the way.

I walked alongside Jordan while following Adrian, thinking about how to save my family from these maniacs. I knew nothing about myself, but I couldn't let them die even after what Jordan said about me.

11 – KANE

"How's your leg, playa," Smoke and I had begun loading our bags in the back of Aasir's taxi. We left the warehouse, figuring it would be too dangerous after the shootout. The General could backtrack and lay us all down. Africa is not our home, so I had to move with caution if we were to survive.

"Shid," Smoke looked down at his leg. "It's straight. Nigga movin', no worries."

"Fo' three," I smiled and threw a playful jab at his chest.

"Fo' two," he blocked the blow. "You know what it is, my guy. Fuck around and be a three-two if I see a cheetah out this hoe."

"I'll be right behind you," I laughed.

"Not without Kim," he joked.

"Shid. . .," I rubbed the back of my neck. "This mufuckin' Africa, Gee. She got legs."

"Ha," Smoke burst out laughing. "You a fool."

"This a whole nother country," I circled my index finger in the air. "You feel me."

"I feel you," we dapped. "Different rules apply."

"Nah," I glanced around the area for Kim. "Let me stop before she sneaks up on a nigga."

"What up with oh boy," Smoke asked, signing with a nod towards Snake. "Talkin' about Abel being crowned the new leader of a rebel army. You just kicked his ass, and I didn't see an army."

My eyes shot over to Snake and Bam, sitting in a left-behind Jeep we took from the warehouse. "I mean . . . who knows. He explained it as if it had just happened. I wouldn't bet on it, though. You know how it is . . . fools talk to hear themselves lie."

"Whatever makes you feel better," he sighed. "I just wanna get this shit over with. It's hot as fuck out here, and it's nighttime."

I tossed the last bag inside and shut the hatch. Smoke wasn't lying. It was hot as hell at 10 p.m. I tried not to think about it. I didn't need anything else to stress over. I joked with Smoke earlier about what Snake laid on us. It did bother me a bit. Abel . . . the leader of an army. He was already a killer. I couldn't imagine him with that kind of power. Jordan had shown up in the nick of time and saved his life. I had Abel, and he got away. I knew this because he wasn't where I had left him. He took a beating that could have ended in death. I couldn't ball my fists for two hours because of the pain. I thought about The Planner finishing him off after I was gone. It wouldn't have satisfied me if someone else had done it.

"Yo," Smoke leaned against the back of the taxi and fired up a blunt.

The rest of my crew were inside the building, getting ready to head out. Snake and Bam sat in the back of the Jeep, waiting for us to move. Doo-Rag's toy soldiers kept a close eye on them. Aasir was sitting in the driver's seat of the taxi, sleeping. After a four-hour drive, who wouldn't be? My man had the nine I gave him sitting on his lap. He was ready to get down if something popped off. "Sup."

"This shit wild, man," he hit the blunt and blew out smoke. "We're in Africa at the same time as Abel, Jordan, and that nigga who shot me. Mom here, Kim, and Bear. A family vacation and shit. Bruh, it didn't hit you that we're beefing with the General of the South African army? Shit, we went from robbin' a bank to war with Africa. Africa, my guy. That's a fuckin' continent. Here . . . hit this and think about it."

I took the blunt from Smoke. Fuck it. I had to clear my mind. My enemies came to Africa, I thought. Not only that, I came to Africa for my enemies. The General was the top priority. I thought about seeing my mother again. I didn't know what the fuck was up with her. She got into some major shit that I had to jump into to keep her safe. If she'd talked to me about the situation, I could have done something. More secrets, I suppose.

12 – RICK

"Noti," her mother shouted.

Aayla heard her mother call Noti's name. She left her room and hurried downstairs to see what she wanted with her sister. She would always be the first to respond. Noti, on the other hand, would come when she was ready. Their mother would give Noti tasks around the house, and Aayla would be the one to fulfill them. She wanted to win her mother's favor. Since Noti was the oldest of the two, she would soon take over the family business. Aayla desired to be in charge, but her mother didn't see her that way, which made her sick. In Aayla's mind, Noti was lazy and not the hard worker their mother thought of her. It was Aayla getting the job done.

Mrs. Wilson watched Aayla come flying downstairs. She shook her head as Aayla stumbled down the last two steps because she was moving so fast. "Slown down before you hurt yourself."

Aayla was out of breath as she shook her head yes in response. "You called, mother?"

Mrs. Wilson looked up the stairs, waiting for Noti to answer. She made a disgruntled face when she didn't appear. "I called your sister. Where is she?" Noti never came when she called for her. It would take at least two or three times for her to come. She wouldn't punish her because Noti was a good child and very smart. When her husband passed away, Noti became distant from the family. "Noti!"

"Mother," Aayla grabbed her mother's arm. "I'm standing right here. Do you need anything from me?" She wanted to prove she was just as good as Noti. Aayla wasn't as close with her father as Noti. She took to her mother instead. She wanted to be as strong and fearless as her. She couldn't understand why her mother didn't see the same fire in her as she did in Noti.

Noti sighed, lying in bed. She heard her mother call the first time but took her time getting up to respond. Her mother called her for any and everything. She wondered why her mother didn't call Aayla. She was the one enjoying life as their mother's personal assistant. She would pass tasks off to Aayla without her knowing about it. She grew tired of the same everyday do this, do that. She wanted to escape but didn't know where to go without her mother finding out. She cried herself to sleep every night, wishing her father was alive.

Mrs. Wilson watched as Noti approached the staircase. The look on her daughter's face told her she didn't want to be bothered. Noti didn't understand why she depended on her. It was time for her daughter to become a woman while she took care of business outside of their home. "Why did it take this long for you to answer me?"

"Mother," Aayla said. "She was sleeping. Let her go back to bed. I can handle anything you need. I can cook and clean."

"Aayla," her mother looked down at her. "I don't need you for anything at the moment. You can go outside and play with your friends."

"But . . .," Aayla was interrupted.

"I said you can go play," Mrs. Wilson eyed her. "Now run along. You can help cook later." She watched Aayla cross her arms over her chest, frustrated as she stomped up the stairs to her room, slamming the door behind her. She sighed. Aayla was a handful. "Bring yourself to me."

Noti rolled her eyes. "Yes, mother." She descended the staircase slowly, pausing between each step.

Mrs. Wilson watched as her daughter approached her side. "Why do you wish to be difficult? I only want the best for you."

"Why do you only call on me," Noti questioned. "You never asked Aayla for anything." She looked away and crossed her arms.

"Noti," Mrs. Wilson put her hand on Noti's cheek. "You act like your father."

"I wish he were here instead of you," she snarled.

Mrs. Wilson backhanded Noti across the face. It sounded like a loud clap, echoing throughout their home. "You will not disrespect me. I am your mother."

Noti's face had turned to the side. She didn't cry or acknowledge the pain she felt. She looked at her mother as if it had never happened. "Sorry, mother."

Mrs. Wilson eyed Noti before speaking. "Take this to Mr. Simmons. He's at his restaurant waiting for you."

Noti took the package from her mother. "Yes, mother."

Aayla listened from the doorway. She cracked it enough to see what was going on downstairs. Noti had to meet Mr. Simmons at his restaurant. It was one of her favorite places to visit because she thought the food was delicious. She left the doorway and slipped on her shoes. Aayla hurried downstairs and passed her mother without saying a word.

"Where are you going," Mrs. Wilson asked as Aayla bolted toward the door.

"To play with my friends."

13 – ABEL

Jordan and I followed Adrian into the town's hotel. Jordan gave me a nasty look as though he wanted to kill me. I kept a straight face. I couldn't show an expression anyhow because of the pain. The women inside had their eyes on us, and so did the men. It could be the way we looked beat up. My face wasn't in the best condition, and Jordan looked like Two-Face from Batman. Adrian walked with a swagger as though he owned the place. I wondered if he'd been here before. We made it to the front counter without a problem. I didn't know if that was a good or bad sign.

"Do you speak English," Adrian rested his arms on the front desk.

I noticed that the soldiers walked inside with several women. They stood around in the lobby, laughing and smoking cigarettes. They spoke in a different language, so I couldn't understand what was said. It did bother me that they came in behind us. I had a feeling they were watching us.

"Yes," I heard the woman at the desk answer Adrian. She had a strong African accent.

"Stop looking around nervously," Jordan nudged me in the side of my stomach with his elbow. "Do you want something to go down?"

I shook my head no and took my focus off the group. I sighed, thinking about going home even though I didn't know where home was. I locked eyes with Jordan and whispered, "I think they're watching us."

"Correction," Jordan turned so the group couldn't see his face. "They're watching the pussy in front of them. They don't give a damn about us, or they would've done something by now, kid."

"I need a room for one night," I heard Adrian in my left ear. "Preferably, on the second or third floor."

"It's obvious we're Americans wearing their uniform," I said in a low tone. "That's a bit suspicious, don't you think?" Jordan and I wore the same exact uniform as the soldiers, which didn't make sense. I didn't want to think about why I wore the same uniform. Adrian, on the other hand, was wearing black clothes.

"No," Jordan responded evenly. "Besides, they're your people."

What, I thought. They're my people? "What do you mean by that?"

"We only accept cash," the woman told Adrian.

"Don't worry about them, prince," Jordan smirked at me. "Their leader is your aunt. They call her Queen Aayla or some shit. Your mother saved our asses by pretending to be her."

Queen Aayla? Before I had time to process what Jordan said, Adrian caught my attention. He'd leaned closer to the woman and said

64

he had no cash, then reached inside his pocket and slid something over to the woman. Whatever it was made her eyes pop out of her head.

"Room 2B," the woman told him. "You can stay as long as you desire." The woman smiled and handed him the room key. "Do you want company tonight?" She smiled.

"That won't be necessary," Adrian responded and took the key. "Please, our stay here is between us. My friends had a few drinks and got into a bar fight. We need to rest. Thank you."

If you call getting shot at with a rocket launcher a bar fight be my guest, I thought. My first thought was she didn't believe Adrian, but she accepted his response. She pointed toward the stairs, and we were off. Of course, why would they have elevators in a place like this? I watched the group unnoticeably through my peripheral version. The soldiers kept their attention on the women, but one happened to glance our way as we walked by. It was an unsettling stare that said eyes were on us.

Jordan spoke to Adrian as we approached the stairs. "Do you always ask for second or third-floor rooms? What are you planning to do? I know you."

I covered my nose because the staircase smelt of piss. The aroma was so awful that I wanted to throw up.

"Hard to climb in," Adrian said. "Easy to climb out."

"Um . . .," Jordan snickered. "The life of a hitman."

I didn't think about it at the time, but Adrian made a solid point. If we were under fire, it would be difficult for someone to climb to the second or third floor without alarming us. They would likely kick in the door and come in as a group. We could quickly jump out of the window and survive the landing.

"What did you give the woman back there that made her want to suck your dick," Jordan asked Adrian.

Believe it or not, but I wanted to now as well. Her eyes grew to the size of walnuts.

Adrian opened the exit door, and we entered the hallway on the second floor. "I slid her a before picture of you."

"Fuck you," Jordan hissed. "What did you give her?"

"Diamonds," Adrian said nonchalantly, searching for the room. "This way."

"What," Jordan erupted. "Are you insane!"

Wow, I thought. Diamonds as a form of payment shouldn't have surprised me after what I had been through, but it did. Every turn with these two became more over the top than the last. I didn't know what to expect anymore.

"Feel free to take them back and give her cash," Adrian told Jordan. "Let's see how that goes for you, loudmouth."

"Where did you get them," Jordan asked.

Adrian found the room and inserted the key. "Does it matter. It's not the one you're looking for."

"It does matter if I'm with you," Jordan said angrily as we entered the room.

Adrian flicked on the light switch and flopped back on the bed. "I did a job in Russia and was paid in diamonds. I carry them with me as a form of payment when I travel. You have nothing to worry about but your face."

"Whatever," Jordan looked at me and then around the room. "There is something to worry about."

"Oh yeah," Adrian shut his eyes. "What's that, cowboy?"

I thought to myself, hopefully, we're only here for one night. I spotted one sofa chair, a desk with a chair, and a single be—

"There's one fuckin' bed," Jordan snatched the thought from my head.

"And," Adrian responded without opening his eyes.

"I can't do this with you right now," Jordan said. "Come with me, kid."

I didn't get a chance to inspect my wounds before it was time to leave again. I followed behind Jordan towards the door.

"Where are you going," Adrian asked.

"To get a med kit," Jordan said over his shoulder.

Great, I thought. He finally said something that made sense.

Adrian held up his hand. "Without the room key?"

Jordan sighed. "Get the key, kid." He walked out the door.

I reached for the key, and Adrian pulled it back.

67

"Don't let him get you into any shit," I'm not sure if Adrian's eyes were cracked open, but that was damn good timing. "Get the kit and come back to the room. We don't need any heat."

"I'm with you," I told him as he held up the key. "The soldiers in the lobby were watching us. What if they want trouble?"

"I'm a trained assassin, and you held your own against me and I had help," he said. "Look at you. You're ten times their size. They won't bother you. You and my brother's face will make anybody stare."

"What about the internet connection?"

"There's a computer in the lobby," he said. "Ask the woman at the desk to use it."

"Ok," I said before leaving the room.

I entered the hallway and didn't see Jordan. Downstairs, I thought. A guy like him doesn't have patience. I got to the door that led to the staircase. I put my hand on the knob and noticed something peculiar. I saw one of the women from the lobby leaning against the wall, just standing alone. Strange, I thought. I shook the thought from my mind and proceeded through the door. She could be waiting for someone. Fuck, the piss aroma hit my nose. I hurried to the bottom of the stairs to escape the smell, and when I opened the door. I bumped into the soldier I saw watching us.

"I'm sorry," I told him. "Please excuse me."

He didn't say a word, just held a nasty expression on his face. He smirked after a long pause, showing off two rabbit gold teeth. He also had a scar on his right cheek. I stood at least a foot taller than him. He looked me up and down as if calculating my size for a fight. I was ready to run after noticing the gun on his waist. I had nothing to protect myself with, which wasn't situational. I did the only thing I could do at the moment. I stood there, waiting for a response, and pretended not to be afraid.

Finally, he said something. "What happened to your face, American?"

Thank God he spoke English. It wasn't the best, but I certainly understood. "Bar fight," I told the same lie Adrian gave the woman at the desk. I thought it would be best that our stories match.

The soldier didn't respond and didn't appear convinced I told the truth.

"He didn't like what I was wearing," I joked, trying to make light of the situation. "I bought this on eBay to piss off the General, so fuck him." I hoped he was gullible enough to believe what I said. If these guys were friends with the army . . . I'm dead.

"Eh," the soldier smiled. "The General and his army can go the hell." He patted me on the soldier and continued up the staircase.

I sighed and walked through the door, thinking if he was heading to the second floor to meet the woman.

14 – RICK

"You're going to Mr. Simmons' restaurant," Aayla said after catching up to Noti.

"No," Noti lied. She kept a decent pace toward her destination.

"I heard mother speaking to you," Aayla threw out there. "You're talking that package to Mr. Simmons."

"Why ask questions when you already know the answer," Noti said evenly. She stopped at the corner and looked in both directions before crossing the road.

Aayla didn't bother checking for vehicles. If Noti crossed the street, then she was okay. "What's in it?" She caught up to Noti and tried to grab the package.

"I don't know," Noti lied, denying Aayla from taking the package. She knew money was inside but didn't wish to tell Aayla. Mrs. Wilson would say to her never mind what's inside. It's not dangerous. Mr. Simmons would open the packages in front of Noti and make her wait while he counted the money. Aayla was unaware because she would roam around the restaurant while Mr. Simmons counted his earnings.

Mr. Simmons' restaurant was within a ten-minute walking distance from their home. Noti had to make this trip twice a week. Aalya would follow her without their mother's knowledge. She never questioned Noti if Aayla was with her, and she didn't bother mentioning it. Aayla was a lot more aggressive than her and had an attitude if things didn't side in her favor. She was more of a tomboy and liked to fight. Noti was the feminine one of the sisters. Fighting wasn't in her nature, but she would if she had to defend herself. However, Aayla was the agitator whenever something went down. She didn't take shit from anyone. No matter how much older or bigger they were to her. This was the same way her mother handled things.

"Why didn't mother ask me to take it," Aayla said, keeping pace with her sister. "I'm old enough and tough." There wasn't a doubt in her mind she could handle whatever their mother threw at her. She desperately wanted to prove that their mother could count on her.

"It isn't your age or toughness," Noti told her as they approached Mr. Simmons' restaurant. She waited to go inside. Aayla would question her until she got an answer. Noti didn't want to enter with Aayla on her back distracting her.

"Then what," Aayla threw up her arms. "I just want to help. I hear you both crying at night because father is gone. I can't sleep anymore because of it. I don't think she loves us the same. You're the special one."

Noti sighed, taking in what Aayla laid on her. Aayla could be hard to deal with. However, she had a soft side, no matter how tough she was. Noti took a second to think about a reply. This was one of those times she had to be the big sister. "Mother loves us the same. I don't want to hear you say that again. I have to take on more responsibility because I'm older. Your time will come when I leave the house." She smiled at Aayla. "I'm sorry for keeping you up at night. I'll try to keep it down."

Aayla smiled at Noti, thinking about what she said. "You want to leave us? Why? Our home is big enough."

"One day, you will want to leave home," Noti pulled Aayla to the side so they wouldn't block the entrance. "You will want to start a family and buy a house. We'll talk about it later. We have to go inside before it gets late. Mother will get angry if we're back in time for dinner."

"Start a family . . .," Aayla scrunched her face. "We are a family."

"Come on," Noti sighed and grabbed Aayla's hand, not before hiding the package inside her jacket. "Mr. Simmons is waiting on me." She opened the door and walked inside, bringing Aayla with her.

There was a small number of people eating with their families. Some of the regulars were recognizable. There were several unfamiliar faces, but she paid them no mind. When Noti first began delivering the packages for her mother. She didn't worry about someone taking the money until she saw what was inside. It took several trips before she stopped being scared for her life. No one would bother her if she minded her business, and Aayla did the same. They were two girls dropping by to pick up food for their mother.

Aalya pulled her hand away from Noti and hurried to the front counter. "Can I please have some curry goat and rice?"

Mr. Simmons looked at Aayla and smiled. She asked for the same meal every time she came into the restaurant. "How are you today, Aayla." He asked while making her a plate.

"I'm fine," Aayla said kindly. "Thank you."

"Hi, Mr. Simmons," Noti reached the counter. "Is she bothering you?"

"Your sister is fine, Noti." He asked and handed Aayla the plate. "How are you today?"

"Thank you, Mr. Simmons," Aayla took the plate.

"You're welcome," he replied with a smile.

"Save some for later," Noti told her. "Mother's making dinner tonight."

Aayla waved her off and sat down to eat at the closest table available.

"I'm ok," Noti told him.

"Are you sure," he questioned. "I know it's been tough since your loss."

"Things are better," Noti lied. "I'm learning to deal with not having him around anymore." She shrugged, revealed the package, and slid it to Mr. Simmons.

Mr. Simmons took the package and didn't bother to look inside. "Son," he called over his shoulder.

Noti thought he would open the package and count the money. That didn't happen. Instead, a young teenage boy came from the back and approached the counter. "Yes, father?"

"I want you to meet Mrs. Wilson's daughter, Noti," he handed his son the package.

The boy turned to Noti. "Nice to meet you, Noti. My name is Jar."

15 – ABEL

I made it to the front desk, and the woman before was not there. I wouldn't blame her if she'd quit after receiving the diamonds. Adrian might have changed her life. I looked around, confused, waiting for someone to show up. I noticed a bell resting on the desk. Great, I thought. I didn't need more attention by alerting the place with a loud chime. I decided to wait for someone to come.

I looked toward the lobby, and the hotel workers were nowhere in sight. Is it dinner time? I thought about walking over to the computer and trying it. The soldiers were gone, and so were the women. Everyone who was in the lobby vacated the area. Standing alone in the lobby felt strange after seeing how active it was fifteen minutes ago. Jordan was missing as well. Nothing made sense. I took and deep breath, thinking it was a coincidence that everyone had left. I thought it feel a bit safer if the soldiers weren't around, but it didn't seem that way.

I walked to the entrance of the building and peeked outside. The only thing in sight was a drunk man and three prostitutes. I didn't see the soldiers or Jordan. Our vehicle was still parked in the same spot. The Jeep was a sign that Jordan was somewhere in the area. What? I spotted another establishment across the road. Something was going on because the place seemed to be live. I shouldn't leave the hotel, I thought. I didn't know anyone other than Jordan and Adrian. Adrian said, lay low, and I sensed trouble would follow if I decided to go. My gut told me to get the hell inside the hotel, fuck Jordan. He's a grown man. I had to look out for myself. There could be others after me, and I didn't know who to watch for. Adrian and his maniac brother were enough of a headache.

I ducked back inside the hotel and to my surprise. The woman from before stood behind the desk as though she had never left. Get out of here, I thought. I casually walked over as if nothing was wrong. "Did the guy with the burnt face pass through here by any chance?" I made a jester with my right hand, signaling to which side of Jordan's damaged face I was referring.

The woman looked confused as if she didn't understand my language. "The nice man in black?"

"No, the other guy," I motioned with my hand again. "Half of his face is burnt."

"No," she said with an accent. "I didn't see a man with a burnt face."

"He's wearing the same uniform," I showed off the rebel uniform to her. "He was with us."

76

She slowly shook her head no. "I don't remember him."

I sighed. I wouldn't get anywhere with her. How could she forget a face like that so quickly? We were just standing in front of her. The diamonds had her mind gone. "Never mind, can I use the computer?"

"Sure," she said. "Your password is 44556-2B. It will operate for thirty minutes at a time. Then you will have to enter it again."

"Thank you," I said before walking away, wondering where she'd gone when I needed assistance. I entered a private area with only a small desk, chair, table lamp, and computer. I took a seat and pressed the power button. It began to boot, and the screen lit. *ENTER PASSWORD* displayed on the screen after a few seconds. I keyed in the code the woman gave me. I gained access, and a small timer began counting down from thirty minutes in the top right corner. I thought this shouldn't take long as I typed my brother's name in the search bar.

Kane Simmons...I pressed enter.

The first link that popped up immediately caught my eye.

FIVE STAR RECRUIT MURDERS TEACHER

The link below read,

JAR SIMMONS FOUND DEAD IN OFFICE

My father, I thought? I read the next link, which was dated two years after the first link.

KANE SIMMONS FOUND NOT GUILTY

I scrolled down the page and found another interesting article.

FBI AGENT LINK TO AFRICAN BLACK DIAMOND HEIST

It didn't stop there.

AGENT JORDAN, MASTERMIND BEHIND ATLANTA MUESUEM HEIST

Everything Jordan told me was true. I found a nice amount of information on Jordan and my brother. I didn't know which article to click on. I sighed, scrolled back to the top, and opened the first article. A mugshot of my brother appeared. I couldn't tell if I resembled him or not because of the condition of my face. He looked awful and mean. I would have thought he did it based on his photo. But who am I to assume anything?

I was stunned after reading the first paragraph about the murder. You have to be a monster to beat someone to death with a baseball bat. He spent two years in jail until he was found not guilty. I could only wonder what I went through during this time. Did I visit him? I know it had to be hard, sitting in jail for something you didn't do . . . or did he?

I gathered as much information on my brother as I could find. After reading ten different articles on Kane Simmons, they got repetitive. I moved on to Jordan. He was a decorative officer with the Atlanta police department and had a great start to his career as an FBI agent. The guy went undercover and brought down the highest-ranking mafia family in America, TMF, which stood for The Mafia Family. His career went uphill from that point on. If you were on the FBI's radar during Jordan's time, you had someone to fear. I would have never thought a manic like him would be saving lives. Jordan's career turned for the worse after my brother was found not guilty. He then worked on the African Black Diamond case in which his partner revealed him as the mastermind behind the heist.

I went back to the article about my father. Someone murdered him, I thought. I clicked on the link and noticed my father was killed the day my brother was released from jail. What a coincidence. There were more photos of Jar Simmons. He was a banker supporting a family of three, found dead. There was an image of him dead in his office. Seeing him lying lifeless on the floor didn't affect me. I couldn't remember anything about him, and he's my father. I wanted to feel angry because someone had taken his life, but I couldn't find it in my heart.

Noti Simmons, my mother. My father chose a beautiful wife. I instantly felt love for her. She had her arm around me in the family photo. The boy with hair was Kane, and my father's arm was around him. They even look alike. I began to feel sick about it and didn't know why. We had a beautiful family. How did we get to this point, I thought.

There was one more person I wanted to search. Abel Simmons . . . I thought as I typed my name into the search bar. I didn't see anything. Not one article featured me. Yale University . . . Jordan said I went there, so hopefully, I could find something on their website. Student inquiry . . . Abel Simmons . . . Wow, I thought. A well-groomed young man appeared. I looked like I was ready to take on the world.

Humph, my brother, and my father had a similar hairstyle, and I chose a baldhead. For what? I smiled, thinking, I do look good with a bald head. I shook the thought from my mind. I attend Yale. I don't want them to see me as something I'm not. That's an excellent reason, Abel. I read my profile. I'm an honors student with a 4.0 GPA. Damn, I am a genius. I didn't feel that intelligent. Did I dumb down after losing my memory? Nah, Jordan and Adrian are dumb.

I found a photo of me with two other students. A guy and a girl. The guy was shorter than me, with a small frame. Maybe he is someone I would befriend judging by his appearance. The girl was okay. She had a short haircut that didn't make her attractive. I wondered how I knew her. She could be the other guy's girlfriend. They looked like they belonged together. I feel like I'm attracted to girls with longer hair.

"Find what you're looking for?"

I heard a voice and felt a hand grip my shoulder. It was unexpected, and I jumped up from the seat, terrified. I took a deep breath and exhaled in relief when I realized it was Jordan. "What the hell, man."

"Pussy," Jordan smirked. "You're gonna get yourself killed acting like that. You're free game."

I put my hand over my chest, waiting for my heart rate to return to normal. "What do you mean?"

"Pussies get fuck," Jordan said. "I shouldn't have to explain that to you, genius."

Whatever, I thought. "I got what I needed on my brother. We're good to move forward." I thought about asking Jordan why he ruined his career but decided against it. "What's that?"

Jordan held up what was in his hand. "Med kit."

"Right," I said.

"Do I need to explain," he said sarcastically.

"I know what it's for," I replied, looking back at the computer and shutting it down. "Where were you? I lost you after leaving the room. Did you go to the place down the street?"

"Did you check the restroom," Jordan pointed to a door. "And what place are you talking about?"

Restroom, I thought. The one place I didn't think to check. "It looks like a hangout spot. Maybe the local bar or something."

"Well then," Jordan smiled. "Let's clean up. I need a drink."

16 – KANE

Bear, Bruce, Bam, and Snake followed behind us in the Jeep. Doo Rag and his crew followed behind them. Bruce decided to drive while Bear sat in the passenger seat and Abel's boys sat in the backseat. Kim, Smoke, and I rode in the taxi with Aasir. My legs got stiff after an hour of driving. I was ready to get out and stretch. There was enough room in the taxi to stretch my legs but it didn't help much. I needed to walk around and get the blood flowing in them. I looked at Kim and she could tell something was wrong.

"Are you ok, baby," she asked.

"My legs are numb," I told her. She put a hand on my right leg and began to massage it.

"Do you want to stop to take a quick break," she asked kindly.

Damn, her hand felt good on my leg. Well, I thought. At least I know the blood is flowing down there. If you know what I mean. "Nah, I don't think we should. I wanna get to where we're going without delay. And I don't want to accidentally bump into trouble along the way because of my legs."

82

"We'll be fine," Kim said. "We've been on the road for over an hour and haven't seen any signs of danger. We should stop and take a second to regroup. The Planner won't be a problem, babe. He would have shown himself by now. The General is gone. You saw what happened. The army left and guys like them don't leave without getting what they came for. They'll die first."

I thought about it and . . . she's right. "Ok, let's take a break." Man, I didn't want to stop. The only thing on my mind was saving my mother. Kim provided a light at the end of the tunnel. My decision-making is off when I focus on one thing in particular. I didn't want to bring Kim on this trip because of the danger. However, I'm happy she's by my side. "Aasir." I leaned forward and called his name. Our eyes locked through the rearview mirror. "Can you stop at the next town? We need to take a quick intermission."

"There is a bar in the next town," Aasir informed me. "They have good food and music. The people there are locals. The army doesn't visit much. The space is controlled by the rebels."

"Let's stop bruh," Smoke looked back at me from the front seat. "My stomach is on E."

"Cool," I said, answering them. "That will work." I turned to Kim. "Are you hungry beautiful?"

Kim smiled at me. "I'm always hungry." She moved her hand over to my left leg and began messaging it. "Are you?"

"Sure," I replied. "I could go some food and plenty of water."

"No . . .," Aasir said. "Don't drink any water. The water in this town is dirty. Drink beer instead. You'll thank me later."

"You heard that bruh," Smoke said. "That's probably why I had to take a shit earlier."

I shook my head.

"Smoke," Kim called. "Dirty water has nothing to do with dropping a deuce. It's all the food you ate at the hotel when we first arrived."

"What's up with the water," that caught my attention. "Is it polluted?"

Aasir looked back at me for a quick second. "You can say that. The rebels throw the bodies of their enemies in the lake." He focused on the road and turned left down a straight path leading to the town. "They call it Blood Lake."

"Blood Lake," I muttered, thinking about bodies floating in the lake.

"Is it safe for us to stop," Kim asked. Her hand paused on my leg.

"The soldiers who visit the town come for three things," Aasir replied while keeping his eyes on the road.

"You know what it is," Smoke said coolly. "Liquor, drugs, and pussy."

"You are wrong, sir," Aasir glanced at Smoke.

"Wha . . . .," Smoke emphasized as if Aasir's response was completely unexpected.

"Food, neutral ground, and rest," I said.

"That is correct," Aasir assured us. "The food is well cooked. The General and his men don't visit the area. The rebels don't have to watch their backs while trying to bump, bump. They can rest at the town's hotel when done with their activities."

"That's tuff," Smoke said.

"The General stays out of the area," Kim spoke up. "Why?"

That's a good question, I thought. The town slowly came into view. It didn't look like the previous town. The buildings weren't destroyed and so far I didn't spot any homeless people.

"If you can't drink the water . . .," Smoke volunteered an answer. "I wouldn't stick around either. Nigga gotta have H20. Ya feel me." He looked back at Kim. "I'm just sayin' sis."

Kim thought about it. "That's not a bad answer."

"You are correct, sir," I heard Aasir over the driver's seat.

"One for two, my guy," Smoke said.

"Apparently, The General likes to drink a glass of water every hour," Aasir continued. "He can't do that here, so he doesn't come."

"That simple," I said.

"This weather with no water," Smoke said over his shoulder. "is a bad combination for brothas."

We entered the town. The road led to a strip of buildings. On the outside of town, small homes surrounded the area. Nothing special but at least they had shelter. There were more bikes and motorscooters than four-wheel vehicles. I began to think who the fuck would want to live in a place where the water is not drinkable? It didn't take long to come up with an answer. They would rather deal with the water situation than the General. That seemed logical to me.

The first thing I noticed was the bar. It was live. I could hear the music as we got closer. Several people were standing outside chatting, minding their business. It was like we didn't exist. It was the first time I didn't feel eyes on me since we arrived and it felt good.

"Babe," Kim grabbed my attention. She pointed a finger away from the bar. "Look over there."

Before I had a chance to see what she was referring to, Smoke spoke in an alert tone. "Al . . . shit. We got action."

Damn, I thought. Four Jeeps were parked on the opposite side of the street, three buildings down from the bar. This can't be good. My mind began to wander. They were the same make and model as the Jeeps at the warehouses. Rebel Jeeps I presumed. Possibly . . . trouble.

"Don't worry about them," Aasir told us. "They are not here to cause harm unless you give them a reason."

"Are you sure about that playboy," Smoke replied. "The last time I saw rebel vehicles shit got crazy."

"I thought you said this place would be safe," Kim asked. "You said they dump their enemies in the lake. Apparently, they come here for four things." She leaned forward and put her hand on the back of Aasir's seat.

"It is safe," Aasir said. "Do you see or hear them?"

Kim sat back. "Maybe it's me." She turned to me and whispered. "I have a bad feeling about this place."

What the hell, I thought. First, she wants to stop for a break. Now, she has a bad feeling. I can't win. "If Aasir says it's safe, we have to trust him. He's been good. Look at how far we've come. Stay by my side. You know I won't let anything happen to you." I kissed her on the cheek and it made her smile. "We'll grab something to eat and leave."

"Ok."

Kim's smile said it all. *Thank you for caring, but it doesn't change how I feel.* That's what I got from it. I found out how to read people at an early age. Mainly, because of Abel. I knew when he got upset. Like the day he didn't get an A plus on his paper. That pissed him off and a teacher paid for it and so did I. Even before that went down. He affected me emotionally. That could be the reason he murdered our father. Could it be he didn't feel loved by him? If you love someone, you don't show it back by taking their life. I chose to spend most of my time with him. Is it my fault? Abel could have done the same. What if I spent more time with him instead of our father? Would he still be alive? I sighed, thinking about what could have been.

We pulled up to what seemed to be the town's hotel. I mean, there is a sign above the door that's barely legible that says Hotel. Aasir parked several spaces away from the Jeeps. I thought about it for a second. I didn't mention anything close to staying the night. "Hey, buddy." I padded his shoulder to get his attention. "Why didn't you park in front of the bar?"

"We're in a cab," Aasir replied. "Someone drunk will try to fetch a ride home. It's better to avoid them. From previous experiences, drunk individuals only understand that this vehicle is a taxi."

"Cool," Smoke said. "I don't mind walking. Hell, I don't park in front of the clubs at home." I heard him open the door.

I watched the rest of our entourage pull in next to us. There was a vehicle on both sides of the cab. I prayed that no one would notice Bear and the others get out of the Jeep. A Jeep that everyone in Africa knew belonged to the rebels.

I turned to Kim before unlocking the door. "Are you good?"

She put on a not-so-happy smile and had the same look in her eyes. "Yes."

I knew it was a lie but no matter what, I wouldn't let anything happen to my heart. There was nothing else I could do to make her feel better besides turning us around to leave. Fuck it, we're here now. "Ok." I put on the same smile and opened the door.

17 – OUR NEXT MOVE

"Why am I still here if you want to help?" Gina had been in the room without food or water for hours. She was beginning to get frustrated with Noti. They spoke earlier for thirty minutes. Noti filled her head with promises of leaving the facility. She contemplated different ideas on how to escape. The chance of getting away was slim to none. Her decision came down to experience. *Why even try,* she thought. There was no way a schoolgirl could manage an escape against a highly trained army. She saw what they could do. The General and his men wouldn't let her get five feet from the facility without shooting her in the head. They could have hunting dogs or field agents, who knows? The best option was to stay put and pray Noti would come through.

Noti didn't answer right away. She casually stepped into the room and shut the door behind her. She understood Gina's frustration. She pulled out a chair and sat in the same spot as before across from Gina. The fire in Gina's eyes told her she was upset. Nothing she could do would please her except for opening the door and walking her to

89

safety. That's what every hostage the General has held prisoner would desire, their freedom.

Gina sighed and closed her eyes before speaking. "Why are you giving me the silent treatment? I thought we were over that?" She began messaging the upper part of her forehead and over to the temples of her skull. She did this to prevent oncoming headaches. "You told me that you would help. It's been hours. I haven't eaten and my stomach is in pain. My mouth is dry. I need water. This is not a good start to our relationship, Noti."

"You can call me, Mrs. Simmons," Noti said polity.

"I will call you Noti until we mutually respect one another," Gina said evenly and opened her eyes.

Noti smirked. *Tough cookie,* she thought. She didn't care if Gina addressed her by first name or Mrs. She didn't need Gina to respect her. She needed Gina for the African Black Diamond. The plan seemed to be developing in the right direction. First, treat her like a mother would a daughter-in-law. Noti wanted Gina to feel as if no one in the could help except for her. Letting Gina go without food or water for hours was one of her tactics. This maneuver she learned from her mother, the real Queen. The Queen deployed this tactic when she needed to extract information from enemies without causing harm. "Whatever you wish."

Gina shook her head slowly unsatisfied with Noti's response. "I'm sure you've eaten and had plenty of water. You get to roam free without restriction. You have an agreement with the General. That part is clear to me. Five hundred million for Aayla and two diamonds or one billion with three. I have ears. I'm not dead . . . yet. Therefore, you value my life. You need the third diamond and this is just a thought . . . the General's father was killed in the Blood Diamond War protecting the third diamond which was the African Black Diamond. He came to America for it so It means the most to him. The Black Diamond is valued at around . . . let's say . . . one hundred million and he's willing to pay one billion for it. Feed me and I'll tell you whatever you want to know and where I last saw it." Gina thought about her current situation. She attended one of the most prestigious universities in the world. It was time to start using her brain.

"There is nothing I need to know," Noti told her. She understood Abel chose Gina because of her intelligence. She'd recalled what Noti told Aayla when they were locked in the cells. She even went as far as breaking down the importance of the African Black Diamond. However, Gina was a bargaining chip in Noti's mind. Other than that, there was nothing significant to know about the diamond or Abel. He murdered his father, her husband, and that was the only thing of importance. "You told me your name and you are Abel's girlfriend. Why would I leave you here? You and my son are in love." Noti smiled. "This facility is well guarded by the army. I just can't walk you out of here. You know the importance of the Black Diamond.

91

Why would he let you leave? I'm doing what I can. You have to trust me."

"How can I trus-" she was cut off by the sound of the door opening. It caught her attention. She looked from Noti over to the entry. Her mouth dropped when a chef stepped passed the threshold holding a plater.

The chef stood next to their table. "Dinner is served." He lowered the platter onto the table in front of them and removed the lid, uncovering a miraculous meal for two.

Gina couldn't speak. The food took her by surprise. *It smells so good,* she thought.

"I thought you would be hungry," Noti glanced at the food and then back at Gina. She knew beforehand the girl would want to eat. If Gina had not mentioned anything about food, Noti would have made her wait until she did. It wouldn't take long, the girl was small. How long could she go without eating something? This was just the start of things to come. "It's called Bazin."

"Bazin," Gina repeated. She was convinced Noti would leave her to die. Not even a second after Noti entered the room, she went off on her. *She got food for me,* she thought. Maybe she could trust Noti. After all, she has yet to speak about Abel negatively. "What's in it?"

The chef spoke up. "The main part of the meal is bread, made by boiling barley flour and salt in water and beaten with a Magraf stick until it develops into a dough which is then baked, served with tomato stew, potatoes, hard-boiled eggs, and mutton."

Gina kept her eyes on the food for a second before looking up at Noti. Her stomach told her to say thank you but her mind said, she's using you. "Thank-"

Noti held up our hand. "Eat, it's not good to work on an empty stomach." She turned to the chef. "Please, leave us."

The chef nodded at Noti and left the room.

Gina picked up a knife and cut the bread. She dipped it in the soup before taking a bit. She closed her eyes, savoring the delicious taste in her mind. It was the best food she'd had since arriving in Africa. Every part of the meal was good. She focused on the food and didn't say a word. Noti's voice made her pause.

"When you're done," Noti eyed her. "I'll take you to meet the General."

18 – RICK

"It was the first time I met Jar," Aayla told Rick. She was sitting on the bed with her back leaned against the wall. It's been years since the memory had surfaced in her mind. Jar meant nothing to her. He ruined her life. The only man she'd ever loved had broken her heart. The pain she felt was unbearable. The only way to fix her heart was the fix the way she viewed men. She learned to see past the lies, their arrogance, and their pride. To her they were only useful in bed, nothing more.

"Mr. Simmons," Rick muttered. His legs began to hurt and he sat on the floor Indian style in front of the cell bars. *A story of heartbreak,* he thought. "The reason we're here. My first murder case. I'm not proud of the results. My partner turned out to be a criminal mastermind and I haven't officially solved the case. Well . . . all signs due point to Abel. He has the African Black Diamond, right? That's what you told your sister. You know . . . I've been trying to locate the diamond for two years. I found it outlandish that I had to travel to Africa in order to track it down. It could be my preposterous way of thinking but the diamond is linked to Jar's sons and the General . . .

and I was assigned to both cases. This is a crazy world we live in, wouldn't you say?"

"Indeed it is," Aayla replied. "How does it feel to lose?"

"What do you mean?" Rick asked perplexed. "I haven't lost yet."

"Americans," Aayla smirked. "Do you think where you're at makes you victorious? You're here because of your pride. Not because of someone else or a case. You put yourself here because you desire to win instead of accepting what was given to you."

"Apparently, that's not how it works in the real world," Rick said. "I'm under oath to protect and serve my country. I have a duty to fulfill as an officer of the law. My job is to –"

"Your job is to value your life," Aayla interrupted. She stood and walked to the bars. "What oath is there if both sides are not obligated to protect? Where are your friends? I don't see any American officers here to save you. You are just one of many casualties they're willing to sacrifice for their gain. Don't fill my ears with foolishness. If you play by the rules in this game prepare to lose."

Rick didn't respond right away. What Aayla said made sense. Ever since joining the FBI, it has been short of sensational. He hasn't received a raise after completing extensive training and moving up to detective. He has been the best in his field since accepting the job. No one has come close to achieving his test scores. To simplify things, Rick outscored his peers ninety-eight percent of the time in twelve different categories. Just when he decided to speak the door opened breaking his train of thought.

"Abtaeid ean alkhalia," the guard said, walking into the holding area.

Rick didn't understand the guard and looked at Aayla for an answer. He watched her back away from the cell bars and sit on the bed. He mimicked her actions figuring it was the correct thing to do.

The guard stopped at his cell. "Abist yadayk, 'ayuha alrajul al'abyad," he tapped the bars with the barrel of his rifle.

"What did he say," Rick looked at Aayla. She smiled and ignored him.

"Abist yadayk, 'ayuha alrajul al'abyad," the guard shouted. "Sa'utliq alnaar ealla rasik!" he aimed the weapon at Rick.

Rick noted the change of tone in the guard's voice. He didn't know what to do. He heard Aayla laughing, offering no help whatsoever. *Think, Rick,* he told himself. What would I want if I were the guard? He concluded and threw up his hands. He figured this one was the most likely answer.

The guard turned away and shouted something at the door. A man dressed in white wearing a chef's hat walked inside holding two trays. He stepped to Rick's cell and slid a tray over to him. He did the same for Aayla and left.

The guard stood in the middle of the room. "Yakul," he said and left the holding room.

Rick had yet to look at the tray. He was too scared to take his eyes off the guard. His eyes traveled down to his feet where the tray was located. He grabbed it from the ground and examined the food. "All that for two slices of bread, an apple, and a juice box." He sighed and sat on the bed.

"Take what you can get," Aayla told him. "You're not in a five-star hotel."

"You could have at least translated what he said," Rick said. "He could've killed me."

"Why," Aayla bit into the bread. "What good are you to me if you can't use your head?"

"You were testing me," Rick asked. "Does this mean we're working together?"

"No," Aayla looked up at Rick. "This means you will live to see tomorrow."

19 – ABEL

"It's just us, shithead," Jordan snarled entering the room.

I stepped in after him and shut the door. I spotted Adrian on the bed. He seemed to be asleep.

"And you call yourself an assassin," Jordan said reacting to Adrian lying out cold in bed as if he'd worked a twelve-hour shift.

"What is that?" I muttered after taking three steps and coming to a stop. I stood there and continued to listen to an unfamiliar sound that I didn't hear before leaving the room.

"What is what?" Jordan turned to my attention.

"You don't hear a faint beeping sound?" I asked while looking around the area curiously.

"What the fuck," Jordan said with his eyes on me.

"I didn't do anything," I told him. This guy is crazy so I had to make it clear to him. There was no telling what he had on his mind.

"Not you," he said. "Move." Jordan pushed me to the side. His attention was on the door.

I looked over his shoulder to see what he was looking at. "What is that?"

"Sonovabitch," he muttered. "He laced the door with C4."

"For what?" Jordan moved from the door, giving me a chance to examine it. This was my first time seeing any kind of lethal explosive. At least this version of myself. "Is he trying to kill us? It could explode while we're asleep."

"The stick is only powerful enough to kill whoever comes through the door," he told me. He sat in the sofa chair next to the nightstand and opened the med kit.

"We just came through the door," I looked back at the C4 and then at him. Every second of the day with these two was life-threatening. My mental state of being was under stress and at risk. These guys want me to have a freaking heart attack, I thought.

"No, kid." Jordan waved me off. "I thought you were smart, but it seems losing your memory has made you dumb. He rigged it to go off if someone forces their way through the door. It's pressure sensitive."

"That explains why he's able to sleep peacefully," I muttered and sat in the chair at the desk. "I guess he is an assassin."

"Whatever," he said.

"That wasn't directed toward you," I said.

"I still heard it," Jordan stood. "I need you to wrap my head."

"What," I said, watching him treat his face.

Jordan held up a roll of self-adherent wrap. "I can't put this shit on myself so I need you to do it. I have a hard time doing shit like this. My fuckin' face is in pain and it will take all day if I do it."

"Ok," I walked over and grabbed the wrap.

"Listen," Jordan said. "Take it easy. I'm a very sensitive man when it comes to my face." He paused. "Wait . . . that didn't come out right."

"I got it," I said. "I want come on the sensitive part of your face."

"You're a fuckin' comedian now," Jordan said. "Who would've known a guy like you would have a sense of humor."

Damn, I thought surprised by Jordan's reaction. I even smiled. I haven't smiled since . . . I couldn't remember the last time I smiled. It's been stressful since we've met. I expected Jordan to flip out like he usually does. Even bad guys take a break from negativity. I wondered if I was funny before the injury. What kind of person I was before Kane and I went at it? Did we get along when we were young? Was I –

"Are you gonna fuckin' do what I ask or what," Jordan asked interrupting my moment of reflection.

I didn't respond. He eyed me for a brief moment. I held a straight face until he broke eye contact. That's strange, I thought. It was the first time he ever looked at me that way. I wanna say he appeared to be . . . scared. There's no way he's frightened of me, I thought. Why would he be? Maybe it was just a feeling I had. It could be me overthinking things that are not likely. I pushed the thought aside and unraveled the wrap. "Alight," I alerted him. "I don't know how much pain you're in so let me know if I'm being too aggressive."

"Just get it over with, kid," Jordan said. "Start at the bottom and wrap around the top. Try not to cover my eyes. I still want to use my gun."

"You got it," I replied.

"Damn, I thought you would think that was funny," he said. "I have to work on new material."

"My fault," I lied, not finding it funny. It felt like more of a threat. "I was focusing too hard on getting this right." I began applying the wrap, holding one end under his chin and bringing it over the top and back down. I continued this process until he grunted. "Too tight?"

"It's good," he said. "Ok, now back to front over my nose and cheeks. Easy. I need to breathe."

"You got it," I did what he asked and locked it in place. "All done. Go have a look."

Jordan walked to the restroom. I didn't follow him. Instead, I opened the med kit and some supplies to treat my wounds. My face wasn't as bad as his but the pain I felt said differently.

Jordan came out and flopped back on the sofa. "You did a good job. Tighten up and we'll head out after you're done."

"You're serious about going to the bar," I don't consider myself a drinker. Well, I didn't feel the need to have one. Besides, I didn't have any money.

"I'm more serious than a heart attack," Jordan said. "Hurry up, it's getting late."

I stepped inside the restroom. This was the first time I got a clean look at my face. It was horrible. I can't believe I walked around looking like this. I turned side to side, examining every bruise and cut. The guy in the mirror staring back didn't look like the Abel I saw on the internet. I barely recognized myself.

I sighed and broke the seal on a tiny packet of Arnicare gel. I decided not to take any NSAIDs such as ibuprofen or Ecotrin. Over-the-counter pain relievers thin the blood and could make the bruises worse. Tylenol would be okay but I left it out as well. The Arnica is a homeopathic herb that is said to reduce inflammation and swelling, thus making it an ideal treatment for bruises. I paused for a moment and thought, how in the hell did I know that? I also know that a 2010 study found that topical arnica ointment effectively reduced laser-induced bruising. What! Slow down, smart guy. My brain decided to tap into my Yale education. Why don't I think on that level all the time? I could have been a doctor. Hopefully, everything will soon come back. But then again . . . I like this version of myself.

20 – KANE

"Big homie," Bruce called over to me after parking the Jeep. "Wassup with the pit stop? I thought we were heading straight to Doo-Rag's place?" I heard him shut off the motor.

"I figured we could use a break to fill our stomachs," I answered Bruce. "At the bar down the street. Just don't drink the water."

"Wha . . .," Bruce had a shocked look on his face.

I shut the door and leaned against the cab. Kim came around the vehicle and stood next to me. I put my arm around her neck and gave her a peck on the lips.

Everyone formed a circle around Kim and me. I explained to them what Aasir told us about the drinking water. I also told them to stay strapped even though Aasir said the town was neutral ground.

"We should not be seen as a mob," Doo-Rag spoke up. "It could bring trouble our way."

"We are deep as fuck," Smoke added. "It's like twenty of us."

"It doesn't look good to me either," Bear said and crossed his arms over his massive chest. "I think we should get a room or two. It's late and we could use some rest."

"You just wanna go to sleep," Smoke said.

"And," Bear replied. "A nigga tired. We just fought a fuckin' army."

"True," I muttered. "What time is it?"

"Five minutes until twelve," Kim answered.

"That's a good idea," Bam unexpectedly spoke up. He looked around the group as if he were one of us. "I agree with him." He pointed at Bear. "We should get a room and get back at it in the morning."

Smoke looked at Bam and lifted his shirt, revealing his weapon. "I'm sure you want to get some sleep."

"If you're thinking I want to use the opportunity to escape, you're wrong," Bam assured him. His eyes went from Smoke to me. "Do you think I have a better chance on my own? We accepted your offer. Snake and I are not dumb. It's our only chance at survival."

I shrugged. "I would love to stay and rest but it's not up to me." I saw the looks on everyone's face. Exhausted, exasperated, tired, frustrated. However, you want to put it but they all needed time to recuperate. I looked down at Kim. "What do you wanna do, love?" I couldn't make that decision without her after what she'd told me in the cab. She didn't feel safe and I'd told her we'd eat and leave. I couldn't go back on my word.

All eyes were on Kim. She took a second, contemplating an answer before speaking. "Ok, this is what we'll do. Doo-Rag, take your crew and Aasir to get a room. Bear, Bruce, and you two." She pointed at Snake and Bear. "Get a room. Kane and I will share a room with Smoke."

"Hell, nah," Smoke broke in. "No . . . way do I wanna hear that shit all night. I'll bunk with the boys."

"Whatever," Kim said. "Three rooms, only for tonight. We'll leave first thing in the morning." Kim reached in her pocket and pulled out a wad of money."

"Damn, sis," Smoke said. "Free bands."

Kim gave the money to Bear. "Get the rooms for us."

Bear took the money. "What about the food?"

"I'll take everyone's order and bring back the food," Kim told him.

"By yourself, sis," Smoke questioned.

"No, silly," she replied. "Let me finish. Kane and Aasir will come with me to get the food."

"I'm not going anyw-" Smoke began.

"And Smoke will come with me to get the food," she said with sarcasm.

"Ok din," Smoke said with a smile. "Shid, you already know."

When Kim finished taking their orders, I took the lead. "We all cool?"

Everyone either shook their heads yes or had a look of satisfaction.

"Smoke," I said. "Go with them to get the room numbers and then find us at the bar."

"Bet," he said.

We set off in different directions. Bear led the way into the hotel with the others. Kim, Aasir, and I headed toward the bar. I kept my eyes forward as we made our way. There were women that I didn't notice before wearing skimpy clothes revealing sexual parts of their bodies. I didn't want to offend Kim by staring but some of them were thick. Bad business for a guy like me. Kim is built the same way. However, these women were on another level. The thickest I've ever seen. Nothing like American women. Good thing my father taught me how to use peripheral vision to keep from distractions such as this occasion. I caught Kim looking at them and it made me smile. She knew I wanted to look. I played it off and she smiled back without saying a word.

We stopped in front of the bar. Several other people were out there standing around chatting, not worried about us. I kept thinking, it's gonna be alright. There was no way in hell the General, Jordan, or Abel would be inside. The General doesn't like the water. Kim shot Jordan with a rocket launcher, and Abel is in critical condition after what I did to him. I'm good . . . right?

21 – ABEL

I shut the door gently as we left the room. I sighed deeply after closing it and turned around to find Jordan inches from my face.

"Stop acting like a pussy," Jordan said. "The damn door won't explode unless you kick it down."

"Just being cautious," I told him.

"Just being a pussy," he said over his shoulder while leading the way to the stairs.

Fuck, I thought. The pissy staircase. I wanted to turn back, but there wasn't another way down to the lobby. The same way up was the same way down. Nothing I could do about it. "How long are we going to be? I would like to get some rest before we hit the road."

"You'll be alright," Jordan told me as he opened the door leading into the staircase. "You don't have a bedtime when you're with me, son."

The piss aroma hit my nose hard. At that very moment, I wouldn't have desired any other thing besides someone thoroughly disinfecting the entire area. If I had cleaning supplies I would have done it myself.

Two flights of stairs, thirty seconds max. That's how long it should take for us to enter and leave the area. Jordan was taking his sweet time. I wondered if he enjoyed the smell. He took one very slow step at a time when he should have been taking three. I came to the conclusion that he wanted to punish me or the aroma reminded him of the projects. Maybe he used to piss in staircases. I should push him, I thought.

I exhaled after exiting the stairs. It felt as though I held my breath for an hour. In terms of reality, two minutes or so. That's a long time without breathing. I shut the door as if someone was after us and it made a loud sound.

Jordan turned to me. "Are you trying to irk my nerves, kid?"

If my mind could answer it would have said, absolutely. "Why would I do that?" I walked past him with a straight look on my face. Jordan was right. I am a pussy. That had to change. I saw the way he looked at me in the room. The fear in his eyes told me somewhere down the line I frightened him. I could be dangerous. He knows I can't remember anything so maybe he's testing me, seeing how far he can push it before I snap.

I heard a faint sound of Jordan sucking his teeth. Of course, I ignored the jester and continued through the lobby. Narcissists seek attention and I wasn't about to let Jordan lure me down that road. I got to the front door and grabbed the handle. Surprisingly, Jordan pulled back on the top part of the handle, keeping me from opening it.

"Listen," Jordan said with a serious look in his eyes. "Don't get there and act as if you're top dog. If you wanna start shit with these motherfuckers, you better be prepared to die. Parading around here like you can't be chopped up and thrown in the fucking woods will only piss them off. So, don't let my arrogance influence the way you act toward them. Take it how you want, kid. At the end of the day, we're on a mission. Don't fucking forget it."

Jordan pushed through the door before giving me a chance to respond. I immediately understood his message and honestly . . . I appreciated it. He noticed a change in my demeanor. My arrogance toward him could get the best of me. What if I'd decided to act in that fashion with the rebels? It wouldn't end well. He didn't come off as disdainful when he said it. That was a respectful warning. It also said he needed me alive. At least for now.

I opened the door and left the hotel. I thought Jordan would have walked further up the road, but I caught him looking curiously around the area. My initial thought was he didn't want me to know he was waiting on me. But it was something more. He faced away from the bar which I speculated to be odd. The action was in the opposite direction.

I stood there until he said what was on his mind. "If you traveled somewhere with your friends. You would park next to them if you were the driver?"

109

"Of course," I said to his back before he turned to face me. "If there was a spot available. I'd take it. And . . . why ask? It's just the three of us."

"How many Jeeps were parked here when we arrived?" Jordan nodded upward toward the vehicles.

"I don't know," I said with a shrug. "Two or three."

"Three," he threw up three fingers and added one. "Four including ours." His eyes inflated, showing that whatever was on his mind was more consequential than the bar.

"What are you getting at?" I pretended not to be worried. Just a few seconds ago he was on my ass and now he's worried about parking spaces. "The whole thing about parking next to friends and the number of vehicles is a bit off-putting."

"Look," Jordan stepped to the side and pointed to an empty parking space. He began to count. "One, two, three, four . . ." he shockingly spun in a full circle and stomped on the ground. "And fuckin' five."

I thought it before and I'm thinking it now. What the fuck is wrong with this maniac? Out of nowhere, he threw a fit like a child counting parking spaces. I didn't know how to react. I stood there puzzled while trying to appear impervious to his actions.

"Five fuckin' Jeeps," he growled. "Five fuckin' spaces. Something isn't right. I can feel it in my bones."

I raised my eyebrows and sighed, all of a sudden, feeling embarrassed. The feeling you get when your child acts up in front of

110

co-workers or when your friend brings up something irrelevant in front of someone of interest. I contemplated between speaking to him like a frat brother or his guardian.

"That isn't the only thing," he pulled out a gun and tapped his head with the barrel.

"Wait a minute cowboy," I held out my arms. Not because I was scared. He was seconds away from getting us chopped up and thrown in the woods for real. I rather get shot. "Put that thing away before you cause unwanted attention. We're supposed to be low-key."

Jordan completely disregarded what I said. "It's parked next to two fu . . . cking minivans. Who would've thought two soccer moms would decide this hotel would be a great place to stay overnight."

"Enough with the sarcasm," I told Jordan. "And put the damn gun away. Another Jeep, so what? You're having a conniption because one guy decided to park next to minivans. And by the way that van is a taxi cab. I'm positive a soccer mom didn't drive that one, but who fucking cares. They didn't come for us. I don't see anybody out here causing a scene other than you. I'm grateful no one is around for this because we'd be dead." Jordan froze and looked at me emotionless. "These guys are focused on the pussy in front of them. Those were your words when I was worried. Well, it seems to me one guy was smart enough to bring two vans full of pussy or he's planning to take a bunch of pussy home. Either way, it won't change our situation. The bar is that way." I pointed back at the building behind me while keeping my attention on him. "Not that way."

Suddenly, Jordan began to laugh. He tucked the gun in his waistband. "You're funny, kid. Smart enough to bring two vans full of pussy or planning to take a bunch of pussy home." He mocked me. "Fuckin' legendary line if I ever heard one." He walked past me, stopped a few feet ahead, and turned around. "Come on. Drinks on me."

I couldn't help but smile at the crazy sonovabitch. "How 'bout that drink." After what just happened. I needed it.

22 – KANE

We stepped inside the bar and I couldn't believe my eyes. It wasn't just any kind of bar. It circled the center of the room. I could order on all sides. The music was very loud and I could barely hear myself think. I kept my arm around Kim, not just to keep her safe, but to let everyone know she belonged to me. This one was mine. Women and men servers were walking around half-naked. I didn't spot one server who was out of shape. The women outside were stacked but the women inside were even more voluptuous. Their breasts and ass were visible. The only part you couldn't see was their nipples. The men were muscular as if they trained before and after work. I wanted to ask Aasir if I should break out a hundred ones. I thought I walked into a strip club.

We followed Aasir through the crowd toward the bar. We headed to the left side. It was the first time I saw rebel soldiers having a good time. Where was that energy at the warehouse? I felt Kim's arm squeeze around my waist, pulling me closer. I looked down at her. She said something but I couldn't make out what. I leaned in with my ear.

"What did you say?" I may have spoken louder than I attended because I felt like I shouted at her.

She moved back a tad. "I can hear you." She came back in. "I said this place is nice."

I didn't want to shout again so I just nodded, letting her know I agreed the place looked cool. I didn't expect nice tables and chairs, and no trash on the floor. My eyes traveled upward and spotted beautiful one-light pendants in different colors hanging from the ceiling. My eyes wandered over to a multi-colored strobe light, hovering over the dance floor, creating a hypnotic atmosphere. Every aspect of the bar appeared to be very well thought out. From the VIP section to the fancy woodgrain countertop in front of me. Someone was making it happen in this small town, making all the money. There wasn't any competition for miles. The last place I saw like this was in Tripoli and it was on the beach.

Aasir turned around as we approached the bar. "This is one of my favorite songs." He smiled and bobbed his head to the beat.

"What do you know about Juve," I look at him sarcastically. When the song came on I couldn't believe my ears. The mood instantly changed and ass was all around me.

"Girl you looks good, won't you back that azz up," Aasir sang along with the crowd.

I couldn't help but laugh because my guy had an accent. Oh shit, my dick got hard as hell. I thought it was because of all the ass in the room. "Get dat shit," I muttered as Kim grinded on my pelvis. It was completely unexpected, but when I thought about it. If there was a song that could change a hostile situation into a Freaknik, this was this song. She put it on me for the next thirty seconds before the DJ mixed in another track. That took a ninja back. Shid, Smoke was right. I'm glad he decided to move into Bear's room. I'm taking Kim to pound town tonight.

Kim closed in on my face. "I had to let them know that you belong to me."

"Fuckin' right," I smirked. Women know women best and so do men. I knew what time it was. All this ass could get a brotha dropped in all reality. I don't care if you're with your girl, wife, or mom. You're gonna catch a fuckin' glimpse of what could have been. It is human nature. "Let's order before shit gets real."

Aasir got the bartender's attention.

A woman strolled over to us. She was one of three women bartenders. I instantly noticed her eyes before her slim thick figure. Her eyes gave off a glow effect due to the UV light, making her seem more attractive. On a scene such as this particular occasion a man's first or second thought without hesitation would be a body scan. It took everything I had not to stare. I kept my eyes locked on hers. Thankfully, she looked at Kim and then Aasir. It could be that Kim and I gave off an *in a relationship,* vibe.

"We're together," Aasir smiled brightly as if he'd been waiting to see her.

"What can I get for you and your friends," She surprisingly didn't have an accent when she spoke.

Kim told the bartender our order and I couldn't believe she didn't write anything down. She popped the caps on three beers and slid the first to Kim, Aasir, and then me. "Are you looking for work?"

I looked at the bartender and smirked casually.

"You're a big guy," she smiled and looked over my arms and chest. "Do you play football?"

"He doesn't play football," Kim interrupted. "I do."

The woman raised an eyebrow with a look of sarcasm. "What team?"

"The only team," Kim followed up quickly.

"The only team," the woman nodded. "I see."

"Can you put in our order," Kim crossed her arms. "It's getting late and I have a game tonight."

"American," the bartender rolled her eyes at Kim before turning away.

"Bitch I'll-" Kim began but I cut her off before she caused a scene.

"Baby," I pulled her closer to me by wrapping my arms around her. This was one of those situations where I had to react immediately. Kim and I have formed a very respectful relationship. She's my end and through her eyes, I'm hers. If this was any other occasion, I'd let them go. Fuck it, catfight. However, it wasn't the time or place. This woman could poison our food. The water is dangerous enough.

Kim regained composure and turned to me while still in my arms. "You heard what she said."

"Babe," my first word toward a white lie. "I barely heard a thing. The music is loud."

"She asked if you play football," Kim made an angry but still cute face. The kind of expression you see on the person you're attracted to and babies. "As if I'm not standing here and she rolled her eyes at me."

"Just about everyone I meet asks that question," I played it to the side, hoping it would calm her down. I know how to talk to my girl. Kim is smart, no doubt. But I have the advantage at certain times. I could be charming and influence her in a mindful direction, depending on the circumstances. Being with her made me realize what my father used to game me on about women. Relationships are nothing but spurts of emotions. We as men, react to the way women feel emotionally and they react to their day. If you treat them well, you only have to react to two; happy and sad.

"But-"

"No buts," figuratively speaking with all the ass around a brotha could get lost. I put my finger over her lips. "Who's playin' tonight? Is it you or her?"

"Me," Kim gave in. She had a disdainful look on her face.

I circled my finger around her lips before placing the tip in her mouth. She kissed it and looked at me seductively. "That's right." I slapped her on the ass.

"Again," she asked.

I slapped it a second time and grabbed it, holding her left butt cheek with my hand. "You feel that?"

"My ass or what's in your pants," when Kim looked up at me, I could've busted a nut. In fact, my father was wrong. There are three affections you should only deal with; happy, sad, and persuasion. With those eyes, Kim could convince me to do anything. My father more than likely mentioned how dangerous a woman can be. I could have missed it because my mother didn't appear to be that way . . . until now.

"Man," I heard a familiar voice. "Nobody wanna see you bake a cake, my guy."

"Smoke," I said coolly and held out my hand. "Wassup."

"Hey, Smoke," Kim waved.

Smoke and I dapped. "Sup dawg, sis." He looked at Aasir. "Pimpin."

"Smoke doggy," Aasir smiled and held out his hand.

"I told you it's just Smoke, my guy," Smoke and Aasir dapped. "You're actin' more and more like a brotha fuckin' with us."

"He could have fooled me," I threw out there. My father told me you're the sum of the five people you're around the most. Aasir had

118

been with us since we met at the airport. It'd been a few days and I sensed his behavior change. "Let Smoke doggy know you're one of us."

"Smoke doggy," Aasir took the time to guzzle his beer. "Brothas come from Africa." He laughed and held his hand out to me. "You're one of us."

I cracked a smile and dapped Aasir. I shook my head at Smoke.

"Brothas come from the hood," Smoke joked. "And brothers come from ya mama."

"You're wrong for that Smoke," Kim said while being unable to hold back a smile. "Don't talk about his mother." She slapped his shoulder playfully.

"Welcome to the Motherland," Aasir shot back.

"Did he take a shot," Smoke said skeptically. "I need one of what he had. That ain't beer."

"One beer, dawg," I said and sat on an open stool. I faced away from the bar. Kim found her way between my legs. Her back was toward me. I wrapped my arms around her waist and kissed her neck.

Smoked slapped down on the counter twice and held out his arm trying to grab the bartender's attention. "I'll take a brewski for me and my dawgz." Smoke signed at us. "Damn, what's your name, shawdy. And you speak good English."

I knew it would be a matter of time before Smoke hopped on something. It was too much ass not to for a single guy.

119

"I only date football players," she said with an attitude.

"Don't you dare," I said in Kim's ear.

She squeezed my arm, holding back her anger.

"Shid, you're looking at a Nigga Fo' Life," I heard Smoke over my shoulder. "Fuck you mean, baby. And I'm from the Motherland. Let her know what it is Aasir."

All I could think was my boy Smoke had done it again when I heard the bartender giggle.

"You're funny," she said.

"You're stayin' with me tonight," Smoke said confidently. "Get three of your big booty friends too. I have two more homeboys. We're staying at the hotel."

"Ok," she agreed.

"My guy," Smoke tapped my arm. "We good on the food?"

"Fosho," I replied.

He turned to the bartender as did I to Kim.

"We good on the food so just the brewskis," he told her.

I heard her pop the bottle caps. Smoke handed them out.

"Don't forget what I said, sexy," Smoke sat in the seat next to us.

"I get off in an hour," she replied.

"Say less," he answered. "I'll meet you in the front with my dawgz."

The bartender had to walk away because Smoke and Aasir sparked up a conversation.

Smoke got my attention by hitting my arm with the back of his hand. "Look who's here . . . fuck."

23 – RICK

"What do you think about Jar?" Aayla asked Noti. "I think he's cute." The girls had just left Mr. Simmons' restaurant and the first thing on Aayla's mind was Jar. She thought he was by far the most handsome boy she'd ever seen. He was tall and his hair was nice. Jar was the only boy she had seen with thin dreadlocks. His hair looked well taken care of, unlike most boys she had come across. Their dreads were much thicker and rough which made them appear mean. He wasn't loud or dirty like the boys she became accustomed to. Jar was different and she couldn't figure out why. For Aayla, it was love at first sight.

"He's ok, I guess," Noti told her. She didn't see what Aayla saw in him just yet. Jar seemed to be soft-spoken. He displayed good manners and was respectful to her. They were the same age and their parents knew each other. Noti decided early on that boys will be boys no matter how they come. She figured the man she'd desired would have to be similar to her father. Jar didn't show any signs of that.

Aayla laughed. "Just okay?" She walked ahead, turned around, and continued walking backward as she spoke. "He's perfect. He's tall and has muscles. Did you see his arms?" She flexed her biceps.

"I saw," Noti said unimpressed.

"His hair, eyes," Aayla continued. "Even his lips. Oh, I love his voice too." Aayla got back in line with Noti just before the intersection. "I have to have him. Jar and I will get married and have kids that look just like father."

Noti looked down at Aayla. "He's older than you and how do you know he wants to marry you? He could be taken. He may not want a bunch of kids running around like you." Noti grabbed Aayla's hand before crossing the road.

"What do you mean," Aayla released Noti's hand just before reaching the other side of the road. She didn't like what Noti told her. If Aayla wanted something, she'd take it. That's what their mother did when she wanted something and Aayla adopted the same habit. You couldn't tell either of them no. "If I want him, he's mine. I don't care if he's older than me or if he's taken. I'm strong like mother, and I will be the last woman standing if I have to fight. You're telling me this because you're jealous." Aayla crossed her arms over her chest.

"Aayla-"

"I have nothing else to say to you," Aayla turned around and marched forward, leaving Noti behind until she reached their doorstep.

She didn't have a key to the house and Noti eventually caught up to her.

"Aayla," Noti started.

"I don't want to speak to you right now," Aayla didn't bother to look at her sister. Noti committed a sin by telling Aayla what she couldn't have which was unacceptable.

"Just listen if you want to see Jar again," Noti used what she could to get very little attention from Aayla. "Don't tell our mother about Jar. You know how she feels about boys. It doesn't matter if he's nice or not. She wants us to stay focused and independent. If you mention anything about a boy she'll find a way to keep him from you which means, she won't let you walk to the restaurant with me again."

"Humph," Aayla kept her face toward the door.

Occasionally, Aayla would act like a baby, and at other times, you would think she was twice her age. She could be difficult, but Noti learned to handle her. "You want to give up Curry Goat?"

Aayla sighed and looked at Noti from the corner of her eyes.

"Okay," Noti unlocked the door as she spoke. "Do as I say." She opened the door and let Aayla enter first. "Mother, we're home."

Aayla hurried upstairs to her room and shut the door hard without realizing her mother standing at the top of the staircase. She was upset with Noti. She wanted Noti to say Jar would like her instead of saying mean things. No one around her was happy. Their mother changed after their father died. She got tougher with them and barely showered

124

them with hugs and kisses. She shouted more and would slap them across the face to keep them in line.

Noti became more emotional. Aayla thought Noti was the little sister because she cried often. She couldn't remember the last time Noti smiled at her. Nothing was the same in the house without their father. She thought she could fix things by helping their mother, showing that she could be the perfect daughter. Although, it didn't seem to matter. Their mother would always resort to Noti if she needed something done.

"Aayla," her mother walked into the room. She stood at the door as she began to speak. "What is your problem and why didn't I see you outside with your friends?"

Aayla sighed and rolled over on her side, facing away from her mother. What was there to say? She couldn't express how she felt about their family or Jar. She wanted to avoid getting shut down twice in one day.

Aayla heard her mother's heels click towards the bed. "Aayla, are you trying to upset me? If you don't wish to speak, you can stay in your room until you do. I don't understand why you choose to behave this way. I only want the best for you and your sister."

Aayla didn't respond. She remained in the same position thinking how different she was compared to Noti and their mother. She heard what her mother said, but her mind focused on the clicking sound from the heels. *Why would anyone wear heels around the house,* she thought. She didn't get why women sacrifice comfort for a particular look. Aayla wasn't girly like Noti and would refuse to participate in girl activities. She despised dresses, heels, and makeup. None of those things would make her strong. Most of her friends were boys. They did things that piqued her interest. Many of their activities required endurance or strength. They played dangerously and she enjoyed it. "You only want the best for Noti."

"What do you mean by that," Mrs. Wilson asked. "That is not true."

Aayla felt her mother on the bed. Shortly after, she felt a hand on her shoulder. "You treat me like a child."

She heard her mother sigh. "That's because you are the youngest. You still have some growing to do. Noti is of age and has to learn responsibility. Your father is no longer with us so Noti has to take on more to help."

Aayla brushed her mother's hand off her shoulder and quickly sat up to face her. "I'm old enough and more responsible than her. I'm strong and fierce like you. I wrestle with boys and beat some of them. Noti has cried every night since father passed and so has you. I cried once." She crossed her arms and held her chin high.

Aayla looked at her mother. "It is okay to cry when you lose someone you love. It doesn't mean you're not strong, honey." She caressed the side of Aayla's cheek. "You're not strong and fierce like me."

Aayla's blood began to simmer and before she could hit boiling point, her mother unexpectedly opened up for the first time since her father's death.

"You're stronger and more fierce than me," she continued with a smile on her face. "Like your father. You are the last of our bloodline and that is only part of what makes you special. You have the blood of a warrior princess. That is something Noti nor I have. You know who you are. Some people never find themselves even through a lifetime of searching. I didn't find myself until your father left us. I was nothing more than a housewife. Now I'm the queen of an empire. I had to change to protect you and your sister. We are who we are because of your father. There is a responsibility we have to uphold." She paused and looked over Aayla. "You should try making your hair look nice and stop fighting with boys. You are a princess." She held one of Aayla's pigtails. "I love you so much."

It was the first time Aayla heard her mother say I love you with conviction. She couldn't remember the last time her mother spoke those words. It had been months. However, they felt meaningful. Showing emotion was somehow difficult for Aayla. It was hard to feel anything. "I love you too, mother." Surprisingly, she got the words out as her mother wiped a single tear that made it to the bottom of her jawline. She didn't realize she had shed a tear. It made her feel vulnerable and weak. She sniffled one time and took charge of her emotions. Vowing to never cry again in front of anyone.

127

Aayla watched her mother walk to the door and turn around. "You went to the restaurant with your sister."

"Are you upset with me?" Aayla asked.

"No, honey," she smiled. "I have a question to ask. . . did your sister meet someone today?"

"Um . . .," Aayla's eyes wandered to the ceiling, confused by the question.

"A boy perhaps," she added, trying to assist Aayla's memory. "At–the restaurant."

"Um . . .," Aayla thought about what Noti said about telling their mother about boys. She would never see the love of her life again. Although she had never lied to her mother.

"It's ok," her mother had a look in her eyes that made Aayla feel she already knew the answer. "Please, I need to know, honey. It's important."

"Yes, mother," Aayla gave in because she still had to prove that she could be trustworthy. "A boy. Mr. Simmons' son, Jar."

"So it's true," she muttered.

"Is what true," Aayla focused on her hands, and when she looked up for an answer. Her mother was gone.

24 – ABEL

We stopped in front of the bar. Jordan turned to me with a serious look in his eyes. "Listen, don't do anything I wouldn't do." Jordan sighed and took the time to scan a well-built woman standing next to the entrance. "Don't fall for any temptations. You need to be at my side at all times. If I go take a shit, you need to be in the stall next to mine taking a shit. Understood?"

I shrugged nonchalantly. "I got it." It surprised me that he would be the one giving orders about keeping cool when he's the one with issues. I didn't see myself as a hothead after losing my memory. The way I've carried myself throughout my encounter with Jordan and Adrian has been nothing short of feeling calm with a bit of nervousness. He should be overly concerned about his actions instead of mine.

"Do you want company tonight," the woman stepped in front of the door, blocking us from entering.

I looked her over. She stood around 5'7 and roughly 140 pounds. Fat in all the right places. Thick thighs and ass. She dressed her face in makeup to appear prettier to the eye. The woman didn't look bad. In fact, she was quite tempting. There wasn't a person on earth who could convince me that she hadn't been passed around the block.

"Do you have your STD test results," Jordan took the prostitute off guard. He had a smirk on his face as he eyed the woman for an answer.

"Honey," the woman said and put her hand on his shoulder. "You have nothing to worry about with me. Come on, you and your friend can join. Half off tonight." She unbuttoned the middle of her shirt, revealing perfect round breasts. She massaged them seductively before lifting them upward for display.

"Maybe some other time," Jordan moved the woman to the side. "Come on, kid." He opened the door and led the way inside.

"What about you, honey," the woman grabbed my arm and placed my hand on her right breast. "I'm clean."

I smiled politely. "I'm fine, thank you."

I failed to realize she kept my hand on her breast. I felt trapped. Her breast was unbelievably soft. I couldn't help but continue to massage it as she smiled back at me. She looked deeply into my eyes as I stood there in a trance. The woman somehow gained access to my brain and took control. I felt my manhood grow. As it got hard I could only think about what it would feel like to be inside her.

"You like," she stood on her tippy toes to whisper in my ear. "I have a place we can go."

The prostitute took my free and caressed her vergina. It didn't register that we were still standing in front of the bar in the open for every to see. She eased my hand into her skimpy shorts. I could feel her clit. It got wet in a hurry as I stuck my finger inside. She moved my hand from her breast and sucked on my finger. That was the breaking point. I couldn't recall ever being with a woman. Especially one who looked as tempting as her. My mind was blank as I continued to please her. I wondered if I'd ever been with a woman. If I had sex or not, or if I'd been in love before. Right then, I decided to explore her.

I backed her up to the building on the side of the front door. She moaned as I forced her backward, pinning her between me and the wall. I knew what she wanted. My middle finger went deeper into her gut, making her moan louder. After a few seconds of pleasuring her, it was time. I removed my hand from her shorts and began to unzip my pants. Suddenly, I felt a hand weigh heavy on my arm.

"What the fuck are you doing," I heard someone shout in my ear.

I ignored the person and continued.

"You're gonna fuckin' kill her," a second cry came from a man.

"Hel . . . lp," the woman in front of me yelp.

What, I thought. My vision became clear. The prostitute looked back at me terrified. Tears filled her eyes as she struggled to free herself from my grip. The hand she used to massage her breast was now around her neck. The tank top she wore had been ripped and tossed to the side. Her hair was now a mess and the makeup had been smeared over her face. I was lost as to what had happened as I came back to reality.

"Let go of her neck," the man on the side shouted.

I turned to the side and saw Jordan tuggling on my arm trying to release the hold I had on the woman's neck. I looked at him confused unaware I was choking the life out of the prostitute.

"Please . . .," the woman cried. "Don't kill me."

"Fuck, kid," Jordan's eyes went from me to the woman. "You're gonna get us killed."

I looked back at the woman and it was then I understood if I didn't release my grip around her neck she could die. "I'm sorry." The woman dropped to the ground and sobbed.

"Dammit," Jordan took cash from his pocket. "Here's fifty for our trouble." He tossed the money on the ground next to the woman.

. "You monster," the woman shouted at me. She coughed several times and spit on the ground while holding her neck.

I stood there, stunned at what I'd done. What's wrong with me? Why couldn't I remember what just took place? I'd blacked out. The last thing I could remember was Jordan walking past the woman into the bar. Everything after that point was vague.

"Shut the fuck up," Jordan snapped at the woman. "Take the money whore!"

The woman picked up the money and threw it in Jordan's face.

"You bitch," Jordan pulled out his gun and pressed it against the woman's head. "Take the fuckin' money and don't say a word. You hear what I said whore!"

"Yes . . . yes," the woman stammered and put up the money.

"Good," Jordan kept on the pressure. "Get up and get the fuck out of here. I don't want to see you again as long as I'm here. Do I make myself clear?"

"Y . . . yes," the woman cried. She stood while Jordan kept the gun pressed against her head.

"Go on now," he slapped her on the ass. "Giddy up." when the woman vanished, Jordan turned to me. "Fuck, kid." He sighed. "I don't want to know what happened. Just don't let it happen again."

"I don't reme-"

"I said, I don't wanna know," Jordan reiterated. "Take the lead. I need to keep an eye on you." He pointed toward the door nonchalantly with his gun before holstering it.

I opened the door to the bar, leading the way inside. Jordan stayed close behind. I could feel him breathing on my neck as I contemplated the recent event. *You monster.* That's what the woman called me. What she said got to me. Who am I? I could be a monster. A man who hits women. Did my father raise me to act that way? I wondered what my mother would think of me. The way Jordan explained her to me it would seem she wouldn't care. I blacked out and took control of that woman. If Jordan wouldn't have shown up, I might have killed her.

133

One-half of me felt horrible for what I'd done. I couldn't tell her enough how sorry I was for hurting her. The other half forced a smirk on my face. A wonderful sensation filled my body as I made my way through the crowd, eyeing every single woman as I passed them by.

25 – RICK

"What happened," Rick took the last bit of his apple and sat it on the tray. He slid it toward the cell bars without getting up from the bunk. Aayla's story had gotten so interesting that it took his mind off food.

"I want to know something before I continue," Aayla stood at the bars after setting the tray on the floor. Her stomach didn't bother her. The food was more than enough. She went days with less. "Why are you still alive?"

It was a shockingly good question. Rick hadn't put much thought into it. *I should be dead,* he thought. What did the General want with him? Noti could have bargained for his life. Different assumptions swirled around in his head. He had put all of his brainpower into making Aayla his ally. Aayla's question deserved a well-thought-out answer and . . . he didn't have one. "Why are you?"

Aayla smirked as though she knew Rick would counter her question. She didn't have to think about a reply. The General had been after her for years and so have her other enemies. "He'll put me on display before taking my life."

Rick shrugged. "He wants to use you as an example. Typical terrorist act." He sighed, pondering the question. *The General wants me alive,* he thought. *Why? I don't have the diamond. Noti took the girl, not me. That would make me useless, right?* Finally, the answer smacked him in the face. He flat-out misunderstood why the General hadn't dismembered his body. "The General thinks he can use me as a bargaining chip with the US because I'm a white American officer. I'm an asset to him."

Aayla didn't respond. She got back in bed and shut her eyes, thinking about her next move.

"He won't get anything for me," Rick laid flat on his back. The twin-sized cotton mattress was hard on his spine. He focused on the ceiling, trying not to fall asleep. It was early morning. He figured around 2 a.m. When Aayla didn't respond, he assumed she wanted to rest. He had to sort things out for himself. Aayla opened his eyes to something. He was being kept alive for a reason. Trading him for another asset seemed ridiculous. There had to be another purpose. "I can't right now." He muttered. Why think of a reason for being alive instead of thinking of staying alive?

I have to make better use of my time, Rick thought. He would have to continue working on his alliance with Aayla. She would be his escape key. Giving up Jordan and Adrian wouldn't get him anywhere

136

other than a grave site. His former partner and co-host didn't have the diamond. Aayla made it clear who had it. Abel. Aayla is the leader of a rebel army and she is Abel's aunt. *Would Abel betray his mother,* he thought. *Why not? He murdered his father.* Aayla's comrades would come for her. Rick had to convince Aayla he could be useful. In the meantime, he needed to get inside her mind. The best FBI detectives studied some form of psychology and Rick graduated at the top of his class.

26 – ABEL

Jordan and I approached the right side of the bar. I couldn't get over feeling horrible for what I did to the prostitute. I shook the recent event from my mind and directed my attention to making it back to the hotel safely. I couldn't blackout like that again. it could mean trouble. It surprised me how Jordan handled the situation. I didn't expect him to pay the woman. I thought he would put a bullet in her head when he revealed the gun, but he just wanted to intimidate her. I'm against hurting women, but I have to say it was good he had my back. No matter how crazy I think he is, at least I'm not alone.

"Two-drink limit," Jordan gestured with his fingers.

The bartender came over after a few seconds. Her eyes were very noticeable. The neon lighting gave them a glow effect. Contacts I presume. She had a nice body as well, slim with a nice backside. She wasn't as thick or attractive as the other women working the bar. She smiled at me politely and I smiled at her which reminded me of the pain lingering in my jaw.

"What can I get for you," she asked, fixing her eyes on me before turning them on Jordan.

"Two double shots of top-shelf and two glasses of water," Jordan told her.

"You got it," she said. "Would that be all?"

"It's a done deal," Jordan leaned on the bar with his elbow. "That will be all for now."

The bartender made the drinks in front of our faces. She kept her eyes on me the entire time. I watched as she poured water from a facet into the glasses. I wasn't sure if they were a shade brown or the water was dirty. Jordan didn't seem to notice because he downed the shot and gulped his glass of water.

"Another," Jordan asked and slammed the shot glass on the counter. He turned to me. "She isn't interested in you. Did you forget what our faces look like?"

The bartender slid him a second shot and he downed it.

I didn't respond to him. My face was in pain and I'm sure it didn't make me out to be the best-looking guy in the building. I took note after entering the place that all of the guy servers were huge and the women had amazing figures. I was bigger than the majority of the men. She could be attracted to my size and not how I look.

"Another," Jordan told her before turning to me. "Stop babysitting."

I took my eyes off the bartender and looked at Jordan. He held up his shot glass. My first thought was the two-drink limit. Jordan was on his third double shot. "You might want to think about slowing down."

"Pick up your glass," Jordan ignored what I said. "We've been through hell. Not that you can recall any of it. No offense." He smiled. The liquor was beginning to take effect. "Your fucking brother. Your fucking mother. Let's not forget his fucking friends."

I slowly shook my head but held up the shot glass to satisfy Jordan while he ranted about all of his misfortune predicaments. I wasn't sure if I ever drank alcohol. After a toast with Jordan, I held the glass to my nose and it hit hard.

"Stop being a pussy," Jordan laughed and downed my glass of water without asking permission. I wasn't gonna drink it anyway. Be my guest. "That hot piece of ass is watching you." He nodded toward the bartender. "It's time to man up."

I took the shot and slammed it on the counter, manning up to impress the woman. "Please excuse my friend. We've been through a lot as you can see." I made a circle gesture with my hand over my face to let her know what I was referring to.

"He's fine," she waved him off. "What is your name?"

"His name is not your type," Jordan cut in. "Another double and a refill of water." He shooed her off with his hand as though she had to travel far.

"Are you sure you want another glass of water," she asked with a concerned expression on her face. "You really shouldn't hav-"

"I want you to fill this glass," Jordan interrupted and tapped the brim of the glass. "I shouldn't have to repeat myself."

She looked at me and I sighed before speaking. "Just fill it. My friend means no harm." I saw Jordan turn toward the crowd. I eyed the woman to get her attention while she made Jordan's drinks. "My name is Abel." I leaned in for her ears only. "What's yours?" I couldn't make the same mistake twice. This was my second opportunity with a woman. Having sex with her didn't cross my mind, I just needed someone other than Jordan or Adrian to conversate with before I went mad.

"Deja," she said with a smile.

"Oh. You have a French name," I said confidently. It didn't stop there. My brain was taking me through one of those episodes where it extracts information from an unknown source I don't have access to. Yale University kicked in. "It means remembrance." I smiled. Not because of her. I smiled because I was absolutely right. I knew that tiny piece of information would blow her mind. It felt crazy not knowing how to be smart when you're a genius.

"Wow," she was stunned by what I said. She reacted the way I wanted her to. "You are the first person who has ever said that to me. You're absolutely right. Wow." She put her hands on her hips, showing off a big smile.

I could see the top and bottom rows of her teeth. They matched the color effect of her eyes. I could have taken it a step further but Jordan decided to ruin the party.

"Ugh . . .," Jordan barfed on the counter and the floor.

I quickly got up to evade Jordan's previous food and liquor intake. I was lucky. Jordan just missed me. I put my hand on his back while he continued to make a mess on the floor.

"Ugh . . .," Jordan was bent over when he looked up at me. He wiped his mouth with his sleeve. "What the fuck is wrong with . . . ugh . . .."

"Is he ok," I heard the bartender.

I took my eyes off Jordan to respond to her. "I don't know. He must have eaten something that didn't mix well with the alcohol. I'll help clean the mess."

She began wiping off the countertop. "It's alright. Just get him to the restroom." She pointed in the direction to take Jordan. "I don't want to lose customers."

"We'll take care of the tab after," she nodded approval and got back to work. I guided Jordan toward the restroom. The people at the bar had disgusted looks on their faces. I could hear them mutter insults our way as I kept Jordan from falling to the ground.

"amsik mashrubak," someone muttered.

"anzur alyh," another went at us.

142

What they were saying didn't affect me. I couldn't understand a word, but I had a general idea of how they felt. I got Jordan to the men's room without a problem. He didn't appear to be drunk when we were at the bar. The attitude had been there so that didn't present any cause for concern.

"My stomach," Jordan cried as I pushed through the door. He coughed several times but nothing came up.

Good, I thought. No one was inside the restroom but us. We didn't need extra attention. There were three stalls and two standups. I chose the stall on the end. Someone would be less likely to stumble into that one.

"Kane, did this to me," Jordan muttered. "Your fuckin' brother is trying . . .," he spat into the toilet. "Kill me."

I locked us in the stall in case I was wrong. Even though it wouldn't seem right to anyone if they found two men together locked in the same stall. Jordan was down on his knees barfing into the toilet. I stood to the side and flushed it to hide the smell. I couldn't take it. Whatever was going on with Jordan wasn't because of the liquor and it sure as hell didn't have anything to do with my brother.

"Where . . . is the sonovabitch," Jordan barfed again. His head was nearly halfway in the toilet. "with my diamond?"

"Kane is not here, Jordan," I made him aware. "It's just us. You're suffering from a sudden illness. Maybe something you ate?" I tried convincing him Kane had nothing to do with his illness. Jordan's confused thinking told me he was delirious. This disturbing state of mind results from illness or intoxication.

Suddenly, I heard the door open. "I thought those guys were gonna be trouble."

"Aasir," another man spoke up. "said this place is neutral ground."

"No of that matters," the other said. "I stay strap."

"Damn, my guy," the man sounded American. The bartender didn't have an accent so I figured another African that spoke very good English. His voice was deeper than the other man. I assumed he was larger than him as well. "You smell that?"

"Hell yeah," the other said. "Shit foul."

"Ugh . . .," Jordan didn't look up. He rested his arms around the toilet, making himself comfortable.

That can't be good. The men had their attention on us. Hopefully, they wouldn't bother us. I needed Jordan to finish so I could get us back to the hotel. It was no longer safe and I couldn't leave him behind. Adrian would kill me which gave me a reason not to.

"You alright in there, dawg," the guy with the deep voice knocked on the stall.

I looked toward the stall as though he would force his way through. I thought about not responding, but they knew we were inside. Something in my brain clicked. It was as if I triggered that section of my brain's defense mechanism. "Je ne parle pas anglais." I told them that I don't speak English in French. Somewhere down the line, I'd learned the language. I found that out when the bartender gave me her name. If they spoke the language we were in trouble. They couldn't know we were Americans. Who knows what they would do to us?

"Bruh," the other spoke up. "Leave this shit alone. We need to get the food and leave. That's what we came here for. I don't know what the fuck he said and it sounds like two mufuckas in there. Little sus."

"I don't understand," the man responded to me. "I'll let someone know you need help."

I didn't say a word. They were going to leave us alone. I looked down at Jordan. Still in panic mode. How did you get yourself into this situation Abel, I thought. A few seconds later I heard one of them turn on the water.

"This water is dirty as fuck," the sound of running water masked his voice, but it came from the smaller man. "Aasir was right. You can't drink this shit."

"I wouldn't wash my hands in it either," deep voice added. "Let's ride."

"Say less," the other agreed. "I'm ready to eat and get on the lil' thing at the bar."

"You a fool," his voice was distant and I heard the door open and shut.

It got utterly silent. It was just us again. I listened carefully and couldn't hear anything but the individuals outside of the door having a good time. I cautiously unlocked the stall and peeked out as if someone was trying to murder me. No one was there. I sighed and turned to Jordan. "It's time to go."

27 – KANE

Smoke got my attention by hitting my arm with the back of his hand. "Look who's here . . . fuck."

Smoke pointed in the direction of the front entrance. I spotted a group of South African soldiers. I couldn't see their faces but I was able to make out their uniform. They were the General's men. Aasir was facing Smoke when I got his attention. He was working on his second beer. "Yo, Aasir. They're cool, right?"

Aasir turned around and took a quick scan of the soldiers. "The General's men."

To me, it sounded like Aasir was shook. "Why are they here? You said the General doesn't bother in this area. Do we need to be concerned?"

"We need to be concerned about those big as guns they're carrying," Smoke throughout there. "I can see them shits from here."

"Let's not panic," Kim spoke up. "For all we know they could be here to have a good time."

147

I noticed Aasir's hands were shaking. It was so bad that the beer bottle in his hand shook. He struggled to wipe sweat from his forehead. I looked at him skeptically. "You ok my man?"

"Hell nah, he's not okay," Smoke replied with his eyes on Aasir. "After all the shit he was talking in the van. Mufuckas came to party for real. It's cool though. We can light this bitch up."

Aasir had a terrified look on his face. He turned to the bar and bumped into Smoke. The mistake caused the beer to accidentally spill on Smoke's clothes.

"Oh, shit," Smoke tried to evade the collision but his reaction time was too late.

"Sorry," Aasir tried to wipe the mess off Smoke's shirt with his hand.

"Chill," Smoke kindly moved his hand. "It's ok." He looked down at his shoes. "At least you didn't get any on my Js."

"You put on new shoes," Kim questioned.

Smoke scrunched his face as if he was shocked Kim would say something like that. "Of course, we're in a public place with fine-ass women. Some of us are single, sis."

Kim shook her head at Smoke.

By this time something on the other side of the bar caught my attention. I couldn't tell what was going on but the people in the area seemed alert. Suddenly, there was enough going on inside the bar I began to worry. "Something's going down over there," I told my crew.

The General's men had my attention along with Aasir panicking, and the commotion on the other side of the bar. I couldn't keep focus on one thing in particular.

Smoke looked in the direction I was referring to. "Yeah, I'm not feelin' this spot. We need to bounce."

"I don't see a fight going on," Kim's eyes were focused on the other side of the bar. "I agree, we need to leave but the food hasn't arrived."

I sighed. Nothing has gone my way since leaving Tripoli. There was always a tough decision I had to face. "Ok, we have no choice but to wait it out," I told them. "No one has started with us, so we're cool and the food should be just about ready." I turned toward the entrance. "It looks like the General's men are being seated in the VIP section which is a good thing. Maybe they are here to have a good time." I looked at Aasir. "You looked worried when you first saw them. Are we good now?"

"Yes," he replied. "I get that way when I see them no matter where I'm at. I had too many bad experiences dealing with those monsters."

"Ok," Smoke spoke up. "Since we gotta be here for a while longer. I need to hit the big dawg's room and clean off. I can't let this shit stain my fit."

"You can't go alone," Kim said. "Go with him, baby. Aasir and I will wait for the food."

"Hell nah," I didn't have to think of a response. "There is no way I'm leaving you alone."

"It's cool," Smoke lifted his shirt. "I'm good, sis."

"No, Smoke," Kim replied. "We need to stick together. This is not the place to be alone." Kim had brought a small Parada purse with her. She opened it and revealed a small 4-shot Derringer. "It ain't much but it will due."

"Whoa," Smoke marveled at the weapon. "That mufucka hard and it's chrome. When you get that, sis?"

"I picked it up when we bought the guns from Doo-Rag," she said. "He gave it to me when were at the abandoned building sorting things out. I figured it could come in handy."

"Alright," I said, stepping in front of her to cover the weapon. "Put that thing away before someone sees it."

Kim did as I said without questioning me.

"At least you brought some kind of protection," I continued. "I'll go with Smoke so he can clean off." I turned to Smoke. "Let's get to it."

"Bet," Smoke led the way to the restroom.

I kept a close eye on our surroundings as we made our way through the crowd. It didn't appear to be chaotic. I scanned the bar where I saw the commotion. Things had settled down. I couldn't see clearly what was going on, but I could see the bartenders. They weren't acting hysterical like most would if a conflict of some kind broke out. I spotted the woman who took our order and she seemed ordinary.

150

I turned my attention to the VIP section. I couldn't see all of the General's men because my view was blocked by other people in the area. Although, I could see a female waitress with a tray of drinks in their section. That gave me some sort of peace. They weren't here to cause trouble. We weren't on their radar. Something I assumed to be very obvious to everyone who noticed them, piqued my interest. They were the only individuals in the bar with assault weapons. It wouldn't play out well if one were to get too intoxicated and decide to air it out. I wondered if it happened before.

I shook the thought from my mind as Smoke pushed through the entrance to the restroom.

"I thought those guys were gonna be trouble," Smoke grabbed some paper towels and stood in front of the mirror, and began whipping himself down.

I stood next to him and looked myself over. "Aasir said this place is neutral ground."

Smoke gave me a look of sarcasm. "None of that matters," he went back to cleaning off his shirt. "I stay strapped."

When we first entered the restroom I didn't smell a thing. Two minutes in a foul scent kept up on me. "Damn, my guy. You smell that?" The smell became so overwhelming that I had to cover my nose. I turned around and looked at the stalls.

"Hell yeah," Smoke stopped what he was doing and looked at me before nodding at the last stall. "Shit foul."

"Ugh . . .," I heard someone who probably had too much to drink.

I looked back at Smoke and he shook his head no. The angel on my shoulder said someone could use my help and the demon on the other said, fuck no. I couldn't help myself so I knocked on the stall gently. "You alright in there, dawg?"

"Je ne parle pas anglaise," a man spoke responded in another language.

I backed off a bit and looked at Smoke skeptically.

"Bruh," he said in a low tone. "Leave this shit alone. We need to get the food and leave. That's what we came here for. I don't know what the fuck he said and it sounds like it's two mufuckas in there. Little sus." He gestured with his hand by holding it flat and then moving it like a seesaw.

I sighed, Smoke was right. I couldn't waste time dealing with something that wasn't my problem. I had too much shit going on to focus on anything outside of that. "I don't understand," I watched Smoke walk back to the counter. "I'll let someone know you need help." Whoever I was speaking with wasn't the same person throwing up. There was no way it was just him in there.

I don't know why I did it but I stepped back about three feet and looked under the stall door. I saw two sets of dirty boots. Rebels, I thought. What confirmed my suggestion was their army fatigue pants. I could see part of their legs. The man I was speaking with was standing next to the guy bent over the toilet. I saw the bottom of his boots. Yep, it's time to fuckin leave.

I heard Smoke turn on the facet. "This water is dirty as fuck. Aasir was right. You can't drink this shit."

"I wouldn't wash my hands in it either," I looked Smoke in the eyes and mouthed *two rebels,* and then pointed at the stall. "Let's ride."

Smoke didn't look at the stall when he mouthed, *told you.* And threw up his hands. "Say less. "I'm ready to eat and get on the lil thang at the bar."

"You a fool," I played it cool to through off the soldiers as we headed for the exit.

We left the restroom and made it back to Kim and Aasir. They were fine. I was thoughtful nothing went down.

"It's about time," Kim said, referring to the two waitresses bringing out our food.

"Hell yeah," Smoke grabbed two of the bags. "I'm hungry as fuck."

"I got it," I told Kim while reaching for the other bags. I winked at her and she smiled back. I gave one of the bags to Aasir. "Time to work, playboy."

"Don't drop that shit," Smoke told him. "You already committed a party foul by spilling your beer on my shirt."

Aasir smiled at Smoke. "I'm ok, Smoke Doggy." He took the bag.

"I'm not the one you have to worry about," Smoke said. "It's the two big mufuckin' grizzlies at the hotel."

153

"Bear is probably hungry as shit too," I added. "And Bruce just left the chain gang. Who knows what he'll do to you." I laughed.

"Stop trying to scare him," Kim looked at Aasir. "Don't listen to them. You should only be afraid if my food is in there." She smiled and led the way out of the bar.

28 – ABEL

"Come on, Jordan," I grabbed him by the arm and tried to lift him from the toilet. "We have to go."

Jordan coughed and spat into the toilet, reluctant to move. "You let him . . . getaway."

"I let who get away," I entertained him while continuing to get him to move.

"Ah . . .," Jordan grabbed his stomach. "Kane."

"Ok, we'll track him down later," I lied just to get him on the same page as me. Jordan was hearing things. The two men whom I spoke with a moment ago had him thinking it was Kane. If it were Kane, I wouldn't think he'd be kind to a random person in a stall. Why would he have time for something minuscule when his problems were major according to what Jordan told me about him? "I need you to stand so I can get you out of here."

Jordan slowly got to his feet. "He'll kill me."

"I won't let that happen," I lied again. If my brother somehow found us. I wouldn't think twice about joining him. My family was

155

more important to me than anything imaginable. I threw Jordan's arm around my shoulder and pushed through the stall door. I looked around suspiciously before heading to the exit. I scanned the area. It was more packed than before. I had no choice but to leave with an open tab. I couldn't drag him back to the bar. That was out of the question.

"That . . . that way," Jordan tried to head back to the bar.

"No," I said. "That's not the way out." Jordan looked me in the eyes as if he wished to speak. His breath was horrible and I turned away, breaking eye contact. I guided him toward the door. Jordan stumbled forward making it difficult for me to carry him. His weight threw off my balance. We resembled two drunk rebel soldiers who needed their legs to hold up a while longer.

Door, I thought. The entrance was just a few more paces ahead. We bumped into a few people and I was thankful they didn't cause trouble. Some of them were surprisingly friendly.

I heard one speak out in English. "Is he ok?"

I kept my attention on the entrance and held up a hand, gesturing that we were fine.

"Do you need help," I heard another.

"We're fine," I said aloud. The music stood over my voice. Hopefully, they heard what I said. I tried to understand why they were being kind to us. This didn't seem like a friendly environment when we first arrived. Just before we reached the door someone I would never expect to see appeared before my eyes. It was the rebel I bumped into on the staircase at the hotel.

"My friend," he said with a heavy African accent. "Let me help."

Before I couldn't refuse his offer he grabbed Jordan's other arm and wrapped it around his neck.

Jordan mumbled a few words. "Who . . . t . . . fu . . . are . . .y."

I'm sure he said, who the fuck are you. He struggled to lift his head toward the soldier so I knew I came close to being spot on. The soldier opened the entrance door and we stepped outside. Fresh air hit my lungs and it felt great. I didn't realize how smoky it was on the inside of the bar. "I got it from here, thank you."

"It's fine," he refused to leave. "We're going to the same place. The hotel, right, my friend."

The man smiled at me, showing off a bottom set of rotten teeth. "Right," I responded sarcastically.

We continued forward. The lower part of my back began to hurt a little. I had to bend over to even myself with their height and the extra load on my neck didn't help. There weren't as many people out as before. It was early and most of them I assume retreated to their domain. I tried my best to keep focus and my eyes on the hotel just ahead of us. It was maybe fifty yards away. I told myself just a little while longer. There wasn't a comfortable bed I could jump into at the end of the road. That belonged to Adrian. My mind began to drift, thinking about how good it would feel to lie down. Sometimes it's the simple things in life that make you feel good.

I calculated the amount of time it took before shit hit the fan. After a minute of shouldering Jordan from the entry, my life flashed before my eyes. We were on the side of the building when it happened. There wasn't a person in site so I couldn't call for help as if someone would show up anyway. Jordan was of no use to me. I was on my own when the rebel decided this would be the location to take what we had and kill us.

"Aetini almas," the rebel shouted after pushing us into a dark ally.

Suddenly, I was taken off guard which was something I should have been prepared for. Jordan's weight disabled my balance and we stumbled to the ground in a few paces. I tripped over bags of trash onto my back and Jordan came down over me. "Ah." Before I could react, there was a gun in my face.

"Aetini almas," the man repeated angrily. His eyes were wide and I could see the hostility in them.

"Kane . . .," Jordan was on his stomach still thinking about my brother, completely unaware his life was in danger.

I held up my hands. "Speak English." It didn't matter what language he used. At the end of this, the problem would remain. I would die and there was no way to prevent or convince the rebel to spare my life.

The rebel put enough space between us to hold out his free hand while keeping the gun directed toward my nose. "I want the fucking diamonds. Give them to me American or die!"

The diamonds, I thought. Adrian's way of payment got us into this unforgivable situation. I could tell him I don't have any diamonds. That would surely piss him off and lead to a face shot. What would Abel do? Why would I think this way? I had to bring out the guy who brought me to Africa. The prodigy who grew up and attended Yale. I don't know why the thought of becoming my former self would get me out of this unfortunate circumstance but . . . it did.

"What happened," I muttered, standing in the middle of the ally. I thought I'd lost my life because for a moment, things went black and my eyes were blinded, flooded in darkness. I searched aimlessly around the area, keeping my head held high, thinking where did the rebel run off to?

"Kane," I heard from below.

Jordan, I thought. I completely forgot about him. I looked toward the ground and not only did I see Jordan lying on top of several bags of trash, but a very noticeable stream of blood leading toward a dumpster caught my eye. "Fuck," I stumbled back and fell against the wall on the opposite side of the dumpster, terrified. It wasn't due to the blood covering the area that frightened me. I'd noticed the rebel's gun was in my hand. The same weapon that was in front of my face moments ago. I dropped it on the ground, wondering how could that be

159

and where had the man gone. My chest panted uncontrollably and an extreme amount of anxiety took over my body. I felt an unsettling dose of nervousness. What did I do, I thought while slowly gathering myself.

I stepped toward the dumpster gradually. Eventually, I passed by Jordan as I approached what could be a murder scene. I wasn't prepared to open the lid on the trashcan. My heart pumped rapidly as if someone had forgotten to turn down the leverage. I contemplated opening it. Did I really want to know what was inside? What if I killed the soldier? Would it change who I am? I'm not sure if I ever saw a dead body. The dumpster was in arm's reach and I stopped just before it and took a deep breath, trying to remain calm. My hands gripped the lid and I shut my eyes like a coward before flipping it open. A strong odor entered my nostrils. The scent was different from what I smelt inside the staircase or the men's room of the bar. This had to be the aroma from something that had died. It could be a dead raccoon, skunk, or any other small animal that was looking for food.

"My God," I finally gained the courage to open my eyes. There he was. The rebel rested on top of the pile. Tossed into the dumpster like garbage. Who in the hell would ever discover the body? It isn't like a garbage truck would come out here. I couldn't fathom one would travel such a long distance for a single pickup. The soldier experienced a single bullet to the head. The right side of his skull was missing which explains the drastic amount of blood loss. His uniform was torn to shreds as if a large beast got ahold of him. My eyes traveled down to his feet. I found it peculiar that his boots were missing. "What the hell happened?"

I couldn't bear to look a second longer. I shut the lid and backed away. After examining the body I came to one conclusion. Someone committed a hate crime while I was out cold. I would remember if I was the corporate. However, the puzzle pieces didn't fit with that assumption. Come on, Abel, think. Trying to convince myself a hero swoop in and save our lives was just outlandish. How ridiculous would this story sound to anyone with common sense?

A dark cloud hovered over me that I had to come to terms with. I horrifically murdered someone. I wanted to ask God for forgiveness for what I'd done. This person couldn't be who I was brought up to become. I wiped the thought of being a murderous manic from my mind. The sky had lightened and the time of day began to show above my head. I needed rest.

I turned around and grabbed Jordan and accidentally kicked the gun that the rebel had drawn on me. It slid across the ground and settled next to Jordan as if it was trying to say . . . kill him. I thought about it as I knelt to pick it up. Blood dripped off my fingertips. I pulled back my right hand to observe it. It was a bloody mess. My left hand didn't match the right. It was clean. I held the rebel by the head with my right hand, I thought. That was the only option I could manifest. I wiped the blood on my shirt as if someone would find out I murdered someone in

161

a back ally thousands of miles away from the US. I went back for the gun. The handle of the weapon was cold in my palm. Chrome .45. I turned it from side to side, looking it over. The clip made a light sound as it ejected into my left hand. Full clip of hollow tip bullets. John Browning invented this masterpiece in 1904 in response to the ineffectiveness of the military sidearm, the Colt M1982 revolver. Information surfaced from my brain that I didn't previously know before now. What was even more satisfying was that it felt good in my hand.

Jordan was still lying over the pile of trash bags, helpless. What would he do without me? I stood over a vulnerable man who needed my help. The same man who desired to do away with my family. Threatened my mother as if it were a normal part of life. I could treat this disease before it infected another human. The only way to eliminate a venomous spread is to kill it. His death would save lives. That's what I told myself as I aimed the gun at Jordan's face and applied pressure to the trigger.

29 – KANE

We left the bar and to my surprise, a cool breeze hit my face. It was the first time the sun was on the opposite side of the earth trying to kill someone other than me. "Damn, you feel that breeze."

"Yeah," Kim stopped in front of Smoke. "It feels good, doesn't it?"

Smoke stepped around Kim. "The hell if I know, sis. You're standing right in front of me. I can't feel a thing."

"Damn," I stood next to Kim and looked at my dawg. " You missed it. Maybe try walking back in and out again." I smiled at him.

"You're being sarcastic, right," Smoke sighed. "I'm light-skinned tho, so it's all good." He laughed and led the way.

"What do you mean by that," I called after him. "Nigga, I'm a shade darker than you."

"Baby," Kim grabbed my right bicep and looked up at me. "You're way darker than Smoke."

I gave her the, yeah, right look. "The blacker the berry, the sweeter the juice."

"What does that mean," Aasir spoke up. "The . . . blacker the berry, . . . the sweeter . . . what?" He seemed to ponder the last part of the saying.

I shook my head. "You wouldn't understand, dawg. It's a black thang."

"I need to know these things," Aasir spoke rapidly.

Before I could reply, Smoke cut in, "Yo . . .."

I took my attention off them and spotted Smoke up ahead. "Come on." I led the way. "He sounds worried." I caught up to him. "Wassup?" He had a shocked look on his face.

"Bruh down there getting his ass torn out the frame," Smoke nodded upward toward the ally.

It was dark out so I couldn't make out their faces as if I knew anyone in Africa besides my crew, Aaisr, and Doo-Rag. Three rebel soldiers apparently had a disagreement. I spotted one of the soldiers lying over trash bags. I couldn't tell if he were dead but he was stiff as a dick in a strip club. Homey had no movement. The other two were going at it. The larger one got ahold of the smaller guy and choked-slammed him. It felt as though the ground below my feet shook. That's how bad it appeared to me.

"What going on," I heard Kim next to me.

"Look," I signaled down the ally. "Buddy down there getting a first-class ass whippin'."

"That's bad," Kim put her hand over her mouth. "They have to be drunk."

"Rebels get into it with their comrades," Aasir spoke up. "They fight over women. It's normal in this town."

"That shit doesn't look normal to me," Smoke said.

I couldn't take my eyes off what was happening. The larger male stood over the little guy and continuously stomped on his face. He was trying to plant his head into the ground. "We should do something." What was taking place shouldn't happen to anyone over a woman. I love Kim but I'm not about to bash another man's face into the ground unless it were Abel. Fighting over a woman in a bar just isn't worth it. There has to be more to the story between the three.

"I tell you what," Smoke replied. "You wanna do something? I got a dub on the big guy. I'll give you ten to one odds."

"I know you ain't trying to bet on the fight, Smoke," Kim turned away. "I can't watch this. Let's go."

"She's right," Aasir agreed. "We need to leave them be. If we intervene. They'll attack us. It's not a good thing to watch either."

"Nah," I couldn't take it any longer. The angel on my shoulder spoke to me again. Telling me I couldn't leave this guy alone. I tuned out everything they suggested and took a step forward, food and all.

"No," Kim blocked me. She laid her hand over my heart. "I won't let you risk getting hurt for three idiots fighting over a woman. You heard what Aasir said."

"Kane," I knew it was serious because Smoke called me by my first name. "Don't let your good heart get you in trouble big dawg. You're my nigga and I got you, but you need to listen to sis. Let's get the fu-"

BANG!

The sound of a gunshot echoed throughout the ally. I wanted to cover my ears but the bags occupied my hands. I reacted by stepping around Kim. If another shot was fired I wanted to prevent her from getting hit.

"Bruh . . .," Smoke didn't have to say another word.

"Let's go," I shouldn't have said those words when I initially saw the men fighting. I let my emotions get the best of me. I couldn't act in such a careless manner while in a foreign country.

"Hurry, hurry," Aasir took off toward the hotel. The man was moving faster than Smoke's forty-yard time.

We all took off. Kim caught up to Aasir with ease. Smoke and I were behind because we were carrying the food. I was more concerned about securing the bags than my back. I couldn't drop this shit. It had been days since we had a good meal.

Kim noticed I wasn't keeping up with the bunch and stopped. She looked at me and waved. "Come on!"

What the fuck do you think I'm trying to do, I thought. I love her with all of my heart but let's be realistic. If I get shot, she'll have a heart attack. If I drop the food and her order is in the bag. She'll have a heart attack. If we're being honest, Kim ran a 4-6 in high school. That's fast as shit for a woman.

Smoke surpassed them and turned around just after Kim. "You good, dawg."

I caught up in less than a second. We were a building away from the hotel. "I'm straight." I looked back to see if the soldier had followed us. We were in the clear. It didn't concern me that we had witnessed a murder. Bodies have been droppin' around me for the past few years. What sat on the edge of my mind was the soldier. He was a very large man. Bigger than any other soldier I've seen besides the General. This guy was around my size. Bruce and Bear were the only men with more mass than me . . . and Abel. It couldn't be, I thought while standing there waiting for the guy to appear from the ally.

Kim grabbed my arm. "Babe."

I knew that it was time to go. I slowly turned around, wishing I could've gotten a better look at the guy and then again. Why would Abel choose to fight a guy in the ally at this time? He's smarter than that. If anything, he's somewhere recovering from the beatdown I gave him and planning his next move. Kim lightly tugged my arm again as if I would go back to help the soldier.

"Kane," I heard Smoke in the background. "It isn't safe out here, dawg. Let's move."

I slowly turned around, still trying to catch a glimpse from the corner of my eye. The guy never appeared. Kim had her hand under my chin and turned my head toward her. I looked down at her, and sighed, leaving what manifested in my mind alone. It was approaching 3 am and we were standing in the middle of a small town in Africa feeling vulnerable. This was the first time I sincerely felt . . . Abel could kill me.

30 – ABEL

"You two walked your asses down to the bar," I looked up at Adrian while shouldering Jordan into the room.

"Is it that obvious," I flopped Jordan onto the sofa chair.

"I told you not to get into any shit," he scanned Jordan. "Fucking idiot can't hold his drink."

"He insisted," I sighed and leaned against the wall. "What was I supposed to do? Let him go alone? You were asleep."

Adrian looked at me with cold eyes. He stood in front of me. The expression on his face said what he was about to say was serious. "What makes you think I'm referring to you idiots drinking at the bar?"

I signed with a confused face. "Then what are you referring to? We went to the bar and came back."

Adrian held his position. I began to wonder if he would attack me. "I referring to the fucking blood on your shirt. You smell like shit and you're not wearing the same boots as before. Is that enough information for your processor, genius?"

169

My eyes dropped immediately down to my feet. What the hell, I thought. That explains why the rebel was barefooted, but why would I take his boots?

"Kid," Adrian grabbed my attention. "Snap out of it. Explain to me what the hell happened. I want to know everything." He pointed to the bed without taking his eyes off mine. "Take a seat."

I had to give Adrian an explanation. He's an assassin who's very observant. The only way to please him is to tell him the whole truth. I stepped past Adrian and sat on the edge of the bed. Ironically, I didn't realize how comfortable the boots were until now. I looked down at my feet, taking a moment to gather my thoughts. Redwing, I thought after seeing an embedded wing with the words *Ring Wing Shoes* across it. Some of the most comfortable footwear in the world. Hump, I thought. I'm fucking crazy. However, my feet were killing me before.

"Well," Adrian crossed his arms over his chest and leaned on the dresser.

"Just trying to recall the night," I replied, looking up at him. "We left the room . . .," I told him everything that happened. Every single detail. It took five minutes to give him a complete summary of what went down.

"So you're telling me," Adrian finally decided to speak after staring aimlessly at me for another two minutes. "It was the water that got this asshole sick?"

"That's right," why would he point that out after all I told him? The five Jeeps, the woman I choked out, the men in the restroom, the rebel in the ally, but yet . . . he's more concerned about the fucking water.

Adrian hurried over to the window and peeked through the blind.

"What up," I asked suspiciously. "Are you concerned about the woman telling the soldier about the diamonds?"

"Not at all," Adrian responded while keeping his attention out of the window. He sighed and turned to me. "Did anyone ask if you came with a woman," he asked. "Another woman perhaps?"

"No," I replied perplexed. "I only got approached by the woman outside of the bar and Deja. The woman at the bar."

"The woman at the bar," Adrian went on. "Did she seem a little . . . too friendly?"

"She's a bartender," I shrugged. "I would imagine they all are."

"Just answer the question," he snapped in a low tone.

"Yes," I said. "I suppose. My face isn't in the best condition so I did find it a bit odd she chose me. I thought she was only being friendly to get us to spend more money."

"Were all of the bartenders, women," he positioned on the dresser, leaning against it with a curious look on his face. An expression he hadn't shown until now.

"They were," I sighed, thinking enough with the interrogation. I wanted him to get to the point. "Three of them."

171

"And this friendly bartender didn't tell you the water was poisoned," he smirked as if it was a joke.

"I guess she tried to warn me," I looked around the room, searching for an answer. "Why would there be poison in the water?"

"Listen, kid," Adrian appeared at ease. "This dumbass has less than a day or two before he's dead. You on the other hand dodge a bullet by not drinking the water."

"The bartender intentionally poisoned Jordan," I asked skeptically.

"I don't think they meant to get him," he put his hand under his chin. "He asked for it by taking the water after being warned by the bartender. There's no reason if you didn't bring a woman into town."

"They," I asked. "Who is . . . they?"

"Casanova," he replied. "He is a major seller of women on the black market. I suspected this was his town when we arrived. They call this place Blood Lake. Every woman here is a prostitute or a worker for him. Those are the ones who didn't fetch a buyer. They use the water to poison males traveling with their women. They get sick and what do you know, there's only one hotel in town. They check in and die within two days. The women are taken hostage and their partners are tossed in the well. Easy pickin'."

"How do you know all this," I was curious to know. The more information I had the better. That's in any situation.

"I'm an assassin," he said evenly. "I'm supposed to know shit like this. My contracts come through the black market. It's not as if I can

172

advertise my services on Google." He shook his head and looked at Jordan. "We have to find Casanova."

"Why," I stood. The weapon I took from the rebel was beginning to hurt my lower back. Leaving it behind would've been foolish. Staying alive was priority number one. "We can't let Jordan die. He's the only way to find my brother." That was the only reason I kept Jordan alive in the ally. I couldn't track down my brother without him. I believe if Jordan dies, Adrian will either leave me stranded or kill me. He doesn't give two shits about finding Kane. He's here because Jordan promised him more money which he would make off the African Black Diamond.

"Finding Casanova is how we save him," Adrian walked to the door and looked over the C4. "He's a former American chemist who fled to Africa to escape prison years ago. I'm one hundred and ten percent sure he has a cure in case of an emergency." He removed the C4. "Stay put and keep an eye on him."

"You're gonna use the diamonds in exchange for the cure," I asked.

"No," he opened the door and turned back. "I'm gonna stick this C4 up his ass and force him to give it to me."

31 – KANE

I sat on the edge of the bed staring off into space. I had my hand wrapped around the back of Kim's head as it bobbed up and down on my manhood. She gobbled half of it down her throat and used her free hand to play with my ball sack.

She pulled out, sucked the sides, and then circled her tongue around the tip. "You like that baby?"

"Yeah," I said evenly.

Suddenly, she stopped and looked up at me. "What's wrong? You're not enjoying it?"

I let out a sigh and lifted her off the floor with ease. She was now standing in front of me ass naked. As sexy as she was to my eyes. My dick went limp. Not because I wasn't attracted to her or anything like that. I couldn't take my mind off the men in the ally. "I'm sorry. It's not you, love. I can't get the rebels off my mind."

"The guys in the ally," she sat on the bed next to me and laid her head on my shoulder.

"Yeah," I looked at her from the corner of my eye. "Fighting over women is one thing but he shot the guy."

"That's one compared to many," Kim messaged my shoulder with her head. "You saw what happened at the warehouse. These guys are crazy. We made the right decision."

"I mean . . .," my eyes traveled toward the ceiling. "you're right. I don't doubt that. It-was the larger guy who caught my attention. He beat that guy to death before shooting him. You have to have hate in your blood to act in that manner toward a comrade. They were fighting for the same cause. Imagine if Smoke and I got into it over you."

"Gross," she slapped me on the back gently.

"Ok," I corrected. "Smoke and Bear got into it over a woman. They're on the same team. A part of the same crew. Even if one had gotten drunk. I wouldn't expect either of them to take it that far. Shit happens. I know everyone isn't built the same, but damn."

"Why does it matter so much to you," she asked rubbing my back with her hand.

I didn't answer right away. My mind wandered back to the scene, recalling everything I saw. "I wish I could have gotten a better look at the guy. He was larger than any rebel we've seen. He was about my size."

"And," she said. "It's genetics."

"Can't be, babe," I shook my head. "The soldiers in the General army are all massive. Guys around my size and up. The rebels seem to

175

be a group made up of misfits. Guys who didn't make the cut. Why would that particular guy play for the wrong team? The way he handled the guy by pummeling his face didn't feel as if he was ever a part of their group. You saw the General's men. They even showed up to the bar. They were massive. You could see the difference in their size compared to the rebels."

"What about the guy waiters in the bar," she countered. "They were in shape."

"They were," I answered. "but they were all smaller than me. They were ripped and their body mass was under 200 pounds. No more than two-ten. I could tell the man in the ally was roughly two-forty, 6'3, 6'4. That's a huge difference."

"One bad apple fell from the tree," she said. "It's nothing to worry about."

I fell back on the bed, keeping my eyes on the ceiling, wondering if I should tell her what was really bothering me. The last thing I wanted to do was frighten her by mentioning Abel's name.

She flopped back next to me and put her hand on my chest. She tapped her fingers repeatedly across it as if she was pondering something. "You think it was Abel, don't you?"

I sighed.

"It's ok," she sat up just enough to look into my eyes. "I'm not worried about him. I have you to protect me . . . and Bear, and Smoke, and Bruce, and Doo-Rag, and those little cute kids who are beyond their age. Nothing will happen to me so don't worry yourself. I've made it this far because of you."

I turned my head towards her and looked deeply into her eyes. I got us to this point safely. Even if it were Abel or just a figment of my imagination. Kim would be in safe hands. No one with me would let anything happen to her.

I cleared my mind to embrace the moment. I put my hand on Kim's breasts and slid it down to her vagina. Damn, she was wet as fuck. I stuck my finger inside and got her ready. I felt her body tense as she looked back at me through passionate eyes.

"Um," she moaned and squeezed my shoulder.

I got on top of her and inserted my manhood. I eased it in so I wouldn't hurt her. Slow strokes at first. Pleasing her was the goal. She closed her eyes and rubbed my shoulders. It felt good to both of us.

"I'm cumming," she whined. "Fuck, it feels so good, baby."

Her grip tightened as I sped up with a growl. "Um," I grunted. A sensation took over my body. I noticed Kim was on edge because her body began to vibrate, signaling it was just about over for her. That was a clear sign that I could end it. She got super wet, making it easy to perform long rapid strokes. Each time I entered deeply, a clapping sound echoed throughout the room. When I realized the end was near for me. I left it in, grinding against her pelvis, trying to push deeper.

"I feel it in my guts, baby," she cried. "Fuck, I'm cumming again. Oh, Kane!"

Take that dick, I thought. Take that fuckin' dick. I kept grinding and after a few seconds. I went back to pounding that pussy until I ejaculated inside her. I assume she came more than three times, achieving an orgasm. It didn't take any longer than two minutes for Kim to roll over and fall asleep.

32 – ABEL

"I want the fucking diamonds. Give them to me American or die!"

I eyed the rebel and signed with a devilish smirk. "I don't have them." I nodded my head toward Jordan. "He does."

"Get them, American," the soldier ordered and quickly signaled at Jordan with it before swiftly refocusing his aim on me. "Now! Don't try anything or I'll shoot you in the head."

"Jordan," I tapped him on the side with my foot, taking my eyes off the weapon. "Give this gentleman the diamonds, would ya."

"Don't fuck with me," The soldier made a mistake and got too close. "I'll fuckin-"

The rebel made a critical miss calculation by moving in arms reach. I quickly chopped his arm that held the weapon and wrapped my free hand around his neck. "You'll fuckin' what?" I grinned, showing off my front teeth. "Die."

The weapon fell to the ground by my feet. I gained the advantage over the simple-minded fool. I squeezed with all of my might, trying to see if I could break his neck without using my other hand. His nails

179

scraped my skin as he struggled to pry my hand away to free himself. I could feel his Adam's apple compressing in my palm, crushing the thyroid cartilage behind it. The color of his eyes changed to a bloodshot red due to vessel breakage. I was getting excited watching him fight to breathe. "Do you want the diamonds as much as you wish to breathe?" I laughed and rushed forward, crashing the soldier into the wall, still maintaining the grip around his neck. His head bounced back after colliding with the brick building.

"...," His eyes grew to the size of walnuts as the chokehold continued to drain the life from his weakened body.

"N'aie pas peur de la mort que tu donnes," I spoke in French, telling him, don't be afraid of the death you give. It is a common rule for murderers to abide by. If you're willing to take a life. You must be willing to accept the same fate.

I sent a powerful blow to his stomach and caused a pool of blood to shoot from his mouth and nostrils unwillingly. I looked at my attire. "You got blood on my hands and uniform, my friend," I repeated the process so many times that I lost count. The rebel was on the verge of death, spitting up an excessive amount of blood and vomit. "How many bones does a normal ribcage have?" I punched the right side of his chest, knowing the excuse for a soldier wouldn't reply. "Wrong answer." I punched the left side even harder, trying to bust through to his thorax. "There are a set of twelve paired bones which form the protective cage of the thorax." Another blow to the right side before

180

continuing the lesson. "They articulate with the vertebral column posteriorly, and terminate anteriorly as cartilage." My fist crushed the left side. The blow might have killed the soldier but I went on, enjoying every second. "Also, known as costal cartilage. You stupid fuck. You remind me of my brother." Thinking about Kane and what he did to me, lit a wick inside my body.

I choke-slammed the small-minded imbecile to the ground and stood over him like a giant. Planting his head in the concrete intrigued me so I tried my very best to do just that. My eyes caught fire as I raised my right foot, imagining Kane was under the boot. I brought hell down on the rebel's face with more than twenty consecutive attempts to achieve my goal. Over . . . and . . . over . . . and . . . over. I was unsuccessful. "You're a fuckin' failer, Abel." I stopped and watched the sky for a brief moment, taking it all in. The air smelt of a thousand years of blood, sweat, and tears. How many people died in this ally, I thought, sighing out of frustration. I looked down at my prey and noticed the weapon. It was a beautiful piece. "Where did you get this masterpiece?" I inspected the gun, making sure the safety was off before aiming at the soldier's head. "Let's see if I can connect with my eyes shut. If I miss, you can live to seek revenge."

I closed my eyes as promised and backed away ten paces. "Dans l'art de la guerre. Un seul peut être vainqueur." In the art of war. Only one can be victorious. I pulled the trigger before opening my eyes. "Hut, Toop, Threep, Fourp; Hut, Toop, Threep, Fourp." I marched

181

toward the soldier and squatted by his side to examine my work. "This one suffered a gunshot wound to the right side of the skull, cap," I joked. "He ain't gonna make it," I scanned the lifeless body which ironically reminded me of my father. I tore off his attire, searching for anything useful. "Thank you," I found a set of keys and put them in my pocket. His vehicle had to be nearby. I noted to search for it later. I ripped open his shirt and spotted dog tags. I snatched it from his neck and read the name engraved on it. "Casanova," I smirked and tossed the chain over my shoulder. I continued my search and found a peculiar green substance in a tiny tube no larger than my index finger. "What the hell is this?" Something told me it was either poison or something else of the sort. You only find shit like this in a science lab. I pocketed it as well.

"What else do you have?" What, I thought, looking at the size of his boots. "You have big feet for a little guy." The boots looked nice so I removed them to check the size. I read the logo on the side, Red Wing Shoes. My feet were aching and I needed a new pair of footwear. "Look at that, size fourteen. You wear my –" I noticed his foot. It was no larger than a size eleven. "Come on, man." However, I understood why he wore them. They were extremely comfortable boots. I slipped them on and stood. Perfect.

I lifted the rebel from the ground. I thought about leaving him but trash belongs in the dumpster. My mother reminded me of that every other day. I'd trash our room just so Kane would have to clean it. After hoisting the rebel over my shoulder. I spotted another rebel lying over a pile of trash bags. Jordan, I thought confused. Why would Jordan be here or did he follow me? Why was I even here? The last thing I remember was . . . The last thing I remember was . . . I couldn't recall how I got here. Fuck, oh well. I'll put a bullet in his head after.

I turned toward the dumpster, walked over, and popped the lid with my free hand. "In you go," I dumped the waste, there, mother. My hands were on the lid, ready to shut the top on the guy when I noticed his face was different. "What," I muttered. The man inside the dumpster was wearing Kane's face.

Suddenly, his eyes opened. "You will never be the same!"

***

I sat up in a panic. My chest was heaving uncontrollably. Sweat poured down my face. "I was dreaming," I muttered. My heart rate shot through the roof. I put my hand over my chest. Every perceptible beat punched the palm of my hand. Jordan was still lying sick in the chair and not dead. I turned to the side and put my feet on the floor. I inhaled deeply and exhaled, trying to calm down. Adrian hadn't made it back to the room. My mind was scrambled with thoughts of deception, but who was I deceiving? Myself, I thought. I stood from the bed and walked into the bathroom. I turned on the water and prepared to splash it on my face. "Poison," I caught myself in the act. I couldn't risk ending up like Jordan. I need fresh air. Adrian ordered me to stay put but I had to do something to get a clear head. Besides, it wouldn't take long. I only needed a minute or two.

I shut the door behind me and hurried down the pissy staircase. Made my way through the lobby, and outside the main door. I stood on the right side of the building, closer to our vehicle, and leaned against the wall. I contemplated if I had actually done what happened in the ally. The dream felt very real. I couldn't imagine I would commit such a harsh crime. I've been proven wrong before. Damnit. I got frustrated, overthinking who Abel was on the other side before losing my memory. I suddenly began to fiend for a cigarette. I'm addicted to nicotine, I thought, patting myself down as if I'd find a pack of Newports. What I did find was a set of keys and a tiny tube filled with a green substance.

184

33 – KANE

I woke up after hearing several knocks at the door.

"Kane, get your ass up," I heard Smoke's voice. "We have shit to do."

What time is it, I thought, looking at the clock on the nightstand. Fuck, it was only 8:45 a.m. I got roughly three solid hours of sleep which wasn't nearly enough time. I rolled over and noticed Kim wasn't by my side. I blinked and rubbed my eyes to rid my blurry vision. I heard the shower running. I sat up and looked at the bathroom door. I wanted to get in with her, but Smoke wouldn't stop beating on the door.

"Yo, Kane," he shouted again. "Get your lazy ass up!"

"A'ight, bruh, chill," I shouted before slowly mustering the strength to stand. I walked over to the door and opened it. "Bruh, it's 7:45 in the morning."

"Nigga, you know it's 8:45," he walked into the room. "Stop playin' wit' me."

"Don't hurt to try," I shut the door and stumbled back to the bed.

185

"Put some pants on, playboy," I flopped on the sofa chair. "Nobody wanna see you in your whitey tighties."

"You got me fucked up," I laughed. "These briefs, play-boy."

"Same shit," he said. "Damn, this chair is comfortable than a mug. The one in our room felt like a brick." He looked at the nightstand. "Y'all still have food left." He reached for it. "Y'all trippin'"

"Be my guest," I slipped on my pants. "I couldn't finish."

"You don't have to tell me why," He'd already dug into it. "I gotta get sis to make this when we get back home." He pointed at it with the fork. "She in the shower."

"Yep," I pulled my shirt down over my head.

"You need to get your ass in there," he didn't look up from the plate. "Clean ya dick, nasty."

"I would have," I eyed him. "but someone decided to wake up extra early." I sat on the bed to put on my socks. "Y'all jump on them hoes last night," I asked. "You have a whole lot of energy."

"Hell, nah," he said with a mouth full. He paused to swallow the food. "Fuck around a past out after crushing my plate. Niggaitis."

"True," I replied. "You probably did yourself a favor."

"Humph," He signed by raising his eyebrows.

I grabbed my J's from under the bed. "You blaze yet?"

"Nah," he finished what was left of the food and sat the plate back on the nightstand. "You tryna burn before we ride?"

"Yeah," I answered tieing my shoes. "I got some shit on my mind."

"Say less," he revealed a blunt. "I twisted one before I came." He ran a flame down the blunt before lighting it. "You good? Is it about the shit that happened in the ally? You seemed concerned about oh boy getting straightened out. He more than likely caught one." He puffed on it and passed it to me.

I grabbed the blunt from his hand and hit it. "Sort of," I blow out smoke.

"What do you mean, sort of," he said reaching for the blunt. "Homes dead. You heard it."

"Yeah," I replied evenly. "It's the other guy that worries me."

He passed the blunt. "What about him?"

"It didn't seem odd he was big as fuck," I hit the blunt. "He was my size."

"He's also bald," Smoke said, taking me by surprise.

"You thought it was Abel too," I don't know why I got excited but my dawg was feeling like me.

"That was my initial thought when I saw them," Smoke hit the blunt hard and passed it. "Shid," he blew out the smoke through his nose. "It was 2 a.m. and next to a bar. Mufuckas get drunk and get down. If you think about it, Abel is fucked right now. We have his boys and the diamond. Sis was with us and one of us could have gotten shot. Why take that risk off an assumption? You feel me."

"Fo'sho," I passed the blunt. "I'm good. Appreciate it. I don't wanna get too high."

187

"Right," Smoke ashed out the blunt. "On another note. I may not be the smartest man in the world, and I know sis IQ is a level above mine." He leaned back on the sofa. "Why is she taking a shower in that dirty ass water? You saw what it looked like in the restroom. The water in our room was brown as fuck, bruh. Shit can't be all that different."

I scratched my head, thinking about what Smoke said. "That's a good fuckin' question," I muttered while standing. I walked over to the bathroom door and knocked. "Bae," Kim usually listens to music while showering. I thought it was strange I didn't hear anything but running water. "Bae," I knocked again and tried to open the door.

"Good, bruh," Smoke asked over my shoulder.

"The door is locked," I said, trying again as if it would magically open. "And I don't hear any music."

"She's been in there for a good minute," Smoke added. "You might wanna check on her."

"Bae," I shouted louder. If she didn't hear me that time something was definitely wrong. I turned to Smoke. "Something up, bruh." I walked over to the nightstand.

"Kick that bitch down," Smoke suggested. "Fuck this hotel." He stood. "You want me to do it?"

"I got it," I grabbed the keycard and went back to the door. Why would you take a shower, Kim? She was better at remembering things than I was. Aasir clearly said the water was polluted and she got her ass in there anyway. You can even see how dirty the water was. I'm assuming she got up this morning and didn't realize how tired she was, turned on the shower without thinking, got in, and past out. She could have gotten sick. Hopefully, she's ok. "Kim," I began to panic. The card was too thick to slide through the crack of the door. I jerked, pulled, and twisted the knob and couldn't get it to open. "She isn't answering, Smoke," I said, hysterically.

"Fuck it," Smoke had a sense of urgency in his voice. "Move, bruh."

I stood to the side as Smoke rushed toward the door and kicked it. "Fuck, my leg." He fell back and grabbed it.

Smoke was high and must have forgotten about his leg injury.

I looked back at him and he waved me off. "I'm straight, bruh. Focus on the door."

I turned around and went to work, slamming my shoulder into the door until I broke through. The steam from the hot water instantly clouded my vision. The bathroom was a small space, sink, and tub-shower combination. I pulled back the shower curtain and my heart fell through the floor. Kim wasn't inside. I looked around confused and didn't spot any signs of her ever being in the bathroom. No towel, no change of clothes, or her favorite shower slippers. Nothing. I put my hands on the top of my head as the world around me began to spin.

Smoke appeared in the doorway. "Sis, ok?"

I looked him in the eyes and he must have noticed the pain in mine.

189

His eyes scanned the bathroom worriedly. "No."

34 – ABEL

I made my way back into the hotel after taking a mental break from life. What I began to realize was the side effects of the accident. I'm experiencing DID, I thought. Dissociative identity disorder which involves switching to other identities. I feel as if someone is taking over my mind. The man I was and the man I am now. Two distinct personalities that represent my change in mood. I have to figure out how to retain this version of Abel.

I sighed walking through the door. My eyes became fixed on the two individuals at the front desk. I stopped in my tracks and focused on Adrian. He had his hand on the side of the woman's face. What is he doing, I thought. It was the same woman he gave the diamonds to for our stay.

Suddenly, he pulled her over the counter. "Where is Casanova!"

The woman was dragged by the ear over the counter onto the floor. "I don't know who you're talking about!" She cried and covered her ear with her hand.

Adrian revealed what appeared to be a sharp dagger. He held the woman down and put the weapon to her neck. "Tell me or I'll slowly slice your throat," he threatened.

I stood at the entry like a block of ice. They had yet to notice me. I took my eyes off them and scanned the area. No one was in the lobby to help the woman. I'm not sure if anyone would help if they saw it. Violence seems to run this place. Deep down in the pit of my stomach. I had a gut feeling that Adrian wouldn't kill the woman. He just wanted information. I got an urge to help her, but I couldn't bring myself to react. Not because it was wrong not to help. Adrian wouldn't stop until he found Casanova. Jordan would die in a matter of hours and the only thing on Adrian's mind was saving his brother. I decided to duck off to the side to prevent exposure. Adrian was unaware I'd left Jordan in the room alone. Not only that, I couldn't tell him that Casanova was lying dead in a dumpster.

"Don't kill me," the woman cried. "I'll tell you what you need to know!" she stopped struggling to get free of Adrian's grip.

"Good girl," he stood and looked down at the woman. "Get up," he skillfully flipped the dagger swiftly in his hand as if he were performing a magic trick.

The woman gradually picked herself up from the floor, keeping her hands visible. I could see in her eyes that she was absolutely terrified of dying. "Casanova has a passage in the basement."

"A passage to where," Adrian lifted the woman's chin high with the edge of the dagger and held up her head.

"It leads to a house," she replied. Her legs appeared to be shaking along with her hands. "where . . . where he keeps the hostages."

"The women he sells on the market," he asked.

"Yes," she stammered. "yes."

"Do you know about the water," Adrian asked calmly. He moved the dagger slowly down to the center of her chest between her breasts.

"Please," the woman said. "Don't kill me. I refused to help with any of the kidnappings. I'm a victim. He murdered my husband five years ago and took my sisters."

Adrian smirked. "Answer the question."

"The water is poison," she said. "There are barrels of pure water in the basement for drinking and showering if that's what you want. Take it."

"Take me to the passage," Adrian ordered. "You can keep the water."

"I can't," she replied. "If anyone sees me in the basement. I'm dead."

"If you don't," Adrian stepped closer. "Well . . . what I'll do to you will be much . . . much . . . worse."

I could feel from where I stood in the shadows that Adrian meant it. The woman shrieked when he closed the gap between them. She nearly made me drool when she mentioned the barrels of water located in the basement, which also brought to mind why the staircase smelt of piss. Casanova didn't want anyone in there for a long period. I assumed it led down into the basement. That's more than likely the reason he gave me a mean look when we first locked eyes. He was protecting his investment.

The woman raised her arm and pointed toward the staircase.

Adrian followed her arm. "Of course," he said and looked back at her. "The stairs as if there's any other way to the basement . . . right."

The woman shook her head no.

Adrian nodded, "Lead the way." He stepped behind the woman and nudged her in the back, pushing her to take the first step. She resembled a baby learning to walk for the first time.

I waited patiently until they reached the door. I wasn't ready to step into the open just yet. Luckily, no one decided to come through the entrance which would have given up my position. The woman stopped at the door and grabbed the knob and held it as if she didn't wish to confront the monster on the opposite side.

"Go ahead," I could barely hear Adrian because of the distance between us.

The woman looked back at him as though she wanted to confirm it was the right thing to do. It was so quiet in the lobby, I heard the knob click when she turned it followed by the creaking sound coming from the door slowly being opened. At this very moment, I realized that I had never seen anyone more terrified than her. Adrian put his hand on her back and guided her over the threshold. They vanished beyond the entryway to the staircase.

I quickly scanned the lobby, checking for any new oppositions that might have caught me off guard. No one was present so I quickly moved from cover. I hurried over to the door, speed walking until I reached it. Most modern doors have a rectangular window, allowing you to view the other side. Unfortunately, this particular door did not. It was time to take a chance. Before I burst through like an idiot, I put my ear to the door and listened for the pair's proximity. I didn't receive any signs of closeness.

I sighed and put my hand on the doorknob. The click of the knob crossed my mind so I gave it a moment before turning it. If I could hear it across the lobby, Adrian could as well. I counted five-one thousand of a second before entering and held my breath. My thumb and index fingers clamped together my nostrils and it didn't stop the piss aroma from invading my sense of smell. Only this time, it didn't bother me as much as before. My focus was on making it down the stairs without alerting Adrian. I looked over the rail and couldn't see up or down. It was a weird setup. Usually, you could possibly see a part of the stairs and if someone was there. That wasn't the only obstacle. No windows or light illuminating the access. It appeared to be a dark tunnel leading to nowhere.

The steps were made of stone. There was no way I could tell if Adrian had stopped or continued onward. I made it down the first flight without a problem. A short pause to listen for activity. I did this for the following three flights to steps. I didn't hear a thing. The structure of the wall turned from smooth stones to rigged bricks, signifying this section of the compound was added later.

". . ."

Suddenly, I heard the woman whimper. I froze midway down the next selection of steps, making my ears available for her cries. I sensed I was close to them. However, I couldn't pinpoint their exact location. One step at a time, Abel. That's what I told myself as the sound of the woman's voice grew near.

What, I thought. The steps turned into a dirt ramp leading further down. The holding rail was also cut off. There was a chance you could look over and fall to your death because there was no support system. The ramp narrowed as I continued forward. Finally, I reached the bottom. The small area was similar to the bottom of a round pit no larger than an average bedroom. Nothing occupied the space but dirt and a very dark tunnel.

". . ." again I heard the woman. This time her cry echoed through the tunnel.

I entered the tunnel, maintaining a steady, cautious pace. Thirty seconds inside, I realized it was becoming harder to breathe. The air was limited due to the lack of a ventilation system. That wasn't my biggest concern. "No . . .," I reached out with my hands and caught the ground, breaking the fall. I tripped over something. Hopefully, Adrian didn't hear me. ". . ." I groaned, rolling over onto my back and sitting up. Dust got in my mouth and I spat several times trying to remove the awful taste. I dusted off while standing, listening, and watching ahead. Adrian hadn't heard my mistake.

I sighed and looked down at my feet. It was dark and what lay in front of me was barely visible. It was a dead body of a rebel soldier. I quickly searched the corps, trying to find something of use. Lighter. I also noticed Adrian took the soldier's weapon. I assumed this man was guarding the tunnel and was defeated by the assassin. I considered not using the lighter but I had to see what was ahead. I removed the .45 I took from Casanove and aimed down the tunnel before sparking a flame, illuminating a very long passageway.

35 – KANE

"Fuck, fuck, fuck," I pushed passed Smoke and went straight for my gun, resting under the pillow. "This shit can't be happening again." I tossed the pillow aside, grabbed my heat, and turned off the safe switch on that bitch.

"Ok," Smoke said over my shoulder. "We don't know if she was kidnapped just yet. Just calm down and get yourself together. She could've left the room on her own. Maybe she forgot something in the whip?"

"Fuck that, dawg," the dread head monster was back in an instant. "Mufuckas 'bout to drop if don't get answers."

"Chill," Smoke held up his hands, trying to calm me. "You just can't go around puttin' niggas in the dirt. It doesn't work like that. Let's check the other rooms and see if one of the others knows where she's at. You know how sis is."

"It does work like that Smoke," I cocked that bitch back and chambered a round. My blood was at an all-time high. "I see one of

198

them niggas and I don't get what I want. It's nighttime, you feel me. Shit 'bout to get real fuckin' dark."

"Ok, bruh," Smoke continued to check my emotions. "Just answer a few questions before you go Dirty Harry on niggas."

"Make that shit quick, bruh," I looked at him, knowing my eyes were wide as fuck.

"A'ight," he agreed. "Tell me what happened last night?"

"Man, fuck kind of question is that," I hurried toward the door. "You're wasting time."

"Kane," Smoke beat me to the door and blocked me from leaving the room. "I can't let you go out there until you have a straight head."

"Get the hell outta my way Smoke," I holstered the gun in my back waistband.

"I can't let you go out there looking for trouble and get yourself killed," he pressed. "Mom dukes need us and if Kim is gone, this isn't the way to go about finding her."

"I'm gonna ask you one more time," I eyed him as if he was the enemy. "Get outta my way."

Smoke sighed and held his position.

"Mufuckas wanna be hard-headed," I nodded with a smirk and lost my fuckin' mind. "Get the fuck outta my way nigga," I grabbed Smoked by the shoulders and pushed him back against the door, pinning him against it. I was furious and he forced my hand. I couldn't let anything happen to Kim. Smoke was in the way of my promise to her. I told her nothing would happen to her as long as I was by her side. I meant what I said. Kim is my heart and soul. She is the reason I'm able to breathe.

"Stop it," Smoked grabbed my shoulders and struggled to hold his position.

I was ten times stronger than Smoke. He didn't stand a chance in a fight by himself. I manhandled him with ease and tossed him toward the ground away from the door. Even though I outweighed him by fifty or so pounds, Smoke was a smart fighter. He held on to the back of my dreads and pulled me down with him as he hit the floor hard on his back. My head jerked awkwardly and twisted my body as I fell on my back as well. "Fuck," I groaned in pain. I watched Smoke spring onto his feet as though he was weightless. "Ah," the mufucka kicked me in the side.

"Fuck is your problem," Smoke said angrily and kicked me again.

I caught his foot and punched his ass in the kneecap.

"Ah," he backed off and grabbed it. "That was a bitch move nigga. You know my shit fucked up."

I jumped to my feet and wrapped my arms around his waist. He didn't have time to react. "You fight like a bitch." I suplexed Smoke's ass with everything I had Hulk Hogan style. The fuckin bed was behind us and I didn't realize until he bounced off it. The maneuver was completely ineffective.

Smoke bounced on the bed like a kid, swinging his arms like Ali. "Just like old times nigga. Come get this shit."

"I beat your ass back then too," I rushed him and lowered my head, trying to spear him. He must've moved because I bounced off of the bed and crashed into the nightstand on the opposite side. The lamp fell off and shattered on the floor. The leftover food stained my clothes.

"Look at your stupid ass," Smoke was by the door after invading me. "Close your mouth when you eat pussy."

"I'm bout to wipe that fuckin' smile off your face," I brushed off my shirt and stood. "Stop runnin' like a hoe and put those hands up with your soft ass."

"Nigga you're soft as baby shit," Smoke shot back. "Fuck you mean. Smoke dawg nigga."

My anger was building fast because we were wasting time. Kim needed my help and yet, here I am fighting my best friend. I walked over to Smoke with my dukes up. "Let's see what you got, pussy."

Smoke balled his fists. "You think you're like that. You don't want these proble-"

I stuck Smoke in his shit before he could finish. "You talk too much."

"Ah," he stumbled back and held his chin. "I wasn't ready. That's some bullshit, bruh."

I didn't want to hit him again but something took over my hands and I landed a shoulder punch. "Stop runnin'."

"A'ight," he eyed me after regaining his footing. "Ah . . .."

Smoke rushed me like a madman and wrapped his arms around my waist. "Let go and fight like a man." I tried to pry his arms apart but his grip was strong. I couldn't break the bear hug. I collapsed my fingers together and came down on his back. His knees buckled but he held tight.

"Yo . . .," someone yelled behind the door.

I couldn't tell who it was but I'm pretty sure they heard us tearing the room apart. Suddenly, Smoke gathered enough strength to rush forward. "Ah . . .," I groaned. My back collided with the wall. It felt as if the wall was made of solid bricks because it hurt like hell. The force shook the wall and an old cheap painting fell off its hook and shattered. It didn't help that I just fought Abel which I was still recovering from. Smoke was putting up a fight that should have ended when it began.

"Kane," I heard behind the door. "What the fuck is goin' on in there. Are you alright!"

"I'm whippin' this nigga ass," Smoke shouted, still holding tight around my waist. "That's what!"

I came down over Smoke's back a second time, bringing him to a knee. "Yeah, nigga." I felt his grip loosen. He couldn't handle another blow like that. He tried to knee me on some UFC shit and it didn't work how he planned. "What the fuck was that soft shit?"

"Open the fuckin' door," I caught the voice. It was Bruce. He banged on the door so hard it shook to the point I thought the screws would fall out of the knob. "I'm bout to bust through this mufucka!"

"Fuck," I shouted in pain. It was a dirty shot but I respected it. Smoke punched me in the side where he knew Abel had stabbed me. "You dirty mufucka." I broke down like an old Buick Skylark. The punch somehow drained all of my power. I felt weak as fuck.

"Hell yeah, nigga," Smoke roared and aimed for the same spot.

"Ah," I took another shot and it felt ten times worse. I gathered the strength to slam down on his back a third time. It was enough force to bring us tumbling to the floor.

I heard the door open by force and slam into the wall. "What the fuck are you two doing?"

Smoke and I wrestled on the floor ignoring Big Bruce. I felt a hand on my shoulder that was stronger than Smoke's strength. Bruce forcefully pulled us apart and I landed roughly four feet away from Smoke. I jumped to my feet ready to get at Smoke. He did the same.

Bruce stood between us with his arms out, separating us. "Yo, chill the fuck out!" He stood his ground as we reached for each other. "Stop it before I get busy on you both." He pushed up apart. "Kane, chill." He eyed me. "Smoke." He swiftly turned to him. "Chill."

I held up my hands and backed off.

"I'm good, bruh," Smoke backed away. "Fuck this nigga," he said before leaving the room.

36 – ABEL

My God, I thought preceding through the tunnel. It's been five long minutes and it didn't feel as if I was advancing anywhere. The personnel who took the time to construct the underground passageway put in enough time and effort to retire. There was no way in the hell anyone could have completed this without an army of men. My legs ached and were getting weaker as if I had been walking for miles. Suddenly, a sign that the end was near came into view. Up ahead was a dim light, barely visible, growing brighter with every approaching step.

"Halt," I heard someone other than Adrian shout.

I hurried forward and slid to a stop. The voice was loud enough to carry into the tunnel. I froze and turned around, thinking the guy was behind me. I continued forward and spotted a large wooden door with a rectangular window with bars. It resembled an 18th-century door modified for a dungeon. Doors like this only exist in the movies, I thought. Good thing I was tall enough to peep through the bars.

I scanned the room on the other side, looking for the woman and Adrian. The first thing I noticed was an impressive amount of 55-gallon drums stacked to the ceiling against every wall side of the room. Surely, they were the barrels of water the woman mentioned to Adrian in the lobby. I grabbed my stomach unaware of how thirsty I had been until now.

". . .," I heard the woman whimper signifying they were close.

I ducked to the side, using the door as a shield.

"Get up," I heard Adrian's voice. I assumed he was speaking to the woman because I didn't hear the rebel's voice or any other commotion. "Move."

I held my position, terrified that Adrian would spot me if I peeped through the bars. There was something about that guy that said he was always watching and aware of his surroundings. You can't be a career assassin without doing so at least that's my perspective.

I took a deep breath. It was amazingly quiet and could hear my heart pounding against my chest. Why am I here? I had to ask myself that question. Some people get into trouble and some people look for trouble. I guess I'm in both categories, hiding behind an ancient door like a fool when my ass should be in the room with Jordan. Way to go, Abel. You are a genius.

I gulped and looked through the bars. No one was in sight. Adrian and the woman were gone. Where is the other guy, I thought. The aggressive voice I heard when approaching the door was surely a rebel soldier. I pondered his whereabouts. I figured his body would sprawled out on the ground dead like the other soldier I came across. "Humph," I didn't have time to think about it. There wasn't a look on the handle of the door. Hopefully, it wouldn't make any weird sounds when trying to open it. Old doors seem to give away someone's presence upon entry. "One, two, three," I pulled the handle back and it was shockingly difficult to budge. How in the hell did Adrian get this fucker open by himself, I thought. The damn door was stuck or something. It felt like I was trying to move a thousand pounds. I tried again and got the same result. I couldn't get the door to move one inch no matter how hard I tried. Adrian must have superhuman strength or the guy on the other side opened it before he died. That had to be the only possibility.

I stepped back and sighed, frustrated. Think Abel. The door doesn't have a lock or any other mechanism preventing me from opening it. I'd scanned the door thoroughly and didn't spot anything as such. I gave it another tug. ". . .," I grunted, putting all of my strength into it. "Fuck," I muttered, getting nowhere. "Just fuckin' open." I slapped my palm against the door and to my surprise, the door opened inward with ease. "Son-ova-bitch," I stood there dumbfounded. Some idiot installed the door backward. The pull handle was supposed to be on the other side. I continued through and checked the other side of the door. It got to me and I had to see the handle on the opposite side.

"Look at that," it was the exact pull-type handle. I shook my head. I guess those were the only handles they had at the time.

"Ok," I turned around to view the basement. "Let's get focused." I walked over to the left side of the room and looked over one of the barrels. I read the label, *Libyian Purified Water*. Just like the woman had said. They were hiding the drinking water in the basement. The people in this town would die for this water if they knew it was here. There wasn't anything else in the basement of interest except a set of stairs leading to another door.

I approached the steps. It was only ten of them made of stone. The door was made differently. It wasn't even close in design to the 18th-century model. This door was modern and sadly, it didn't have a see-through window or bars. The surface was solid, preventing a view of the other side.

I ascended the steps and before opening it, I put my ear to the door and listened for any signs of activity. I figured the door was soundproof because I couldn't hear anything. I was well aware the door led into a house where Casanova kept hostages. Adrian spoke the me about women trafficking on the black market and the woman gave him the location in the lobby, hoping Adrian would spare her life. My mind began to drift. I thought about how many women could be in the house and . . . if I could save them. It was painful thinking about innocent women being taken advantage of. Sadly, I knew there wasn't anything I could do to help.

I shook the thought out of my head. I had to think of a way to get on the other side without being noticed. Even someone as intelligent as me couldn't figure this out. I came to a conclusion. Instead of using all of my brain power on something that could one hundred percent end badly. I just dumbed down and lightly knocked on the door. Smart or dumb, same result. It's a door. The only way to tell if someone was on the other side was to just knock. The worst outcome would be Adrian answering and if that were to happen, maybe I could convince him not to take off my head.

I tapped on the door three more times. No one answered. Here you go again, taking chances, I thought while turning the knob. The door creaked, but it didn't worry me. It wasn't loud enough to alert anyone. The triple tap on the door was noisier. I gently eased the door open just enough to observe the right side of the room. I was staring into a kitchen. A dining set and a refrigerator came into view. I paused, checking for sounds of movement. Nothing. I sighed and opened the door fully.

I stuck my head through first, praying it would remain intact. The kitchen was surprisingly clean. You could eat off of the floor and I wouldn't say it just to say it. Shit, I thought. Casanova was living like a king. The dining room table was long with four chairs on each side and one at each end. My view was cut off so I didn't notice the actual length until now. Marbel, I thought, looking at the floor and countertops. Stainless steel refrigerator and microwave. Pots and pans hung above an island-style stove. Who the fuck lives here, Gordon Ramsay?

The setup didn't resemble any place to keep hostages. I guess being kidnapped by Casanova comes with certain perks. I mean, he is a ladies man. What other way to impress a woman than by having a nice home?

I crept into the kitchen, exposing myself to danger. The kitchen opened into a massive elegant living room area. The furniture was probably worth more than a Ferrari. I spotted a rare painting on the wall above an elaborate fireplace. *The Concert,* I thought. No fuckin' way that's the real thing. In Boston on March 18, 1990, a group of thieves stole 13 pieces, collectively $500 million, from the Isabella Stewart Gardner Museum. Among the pieces stolen was Vermeer's The Concert, which is considered to be the most valuable stolen painting in the world. A reward of $10 million is still offered for information leading to its return. Damn, I was doing it again. I shouldn't get on myself for being smart. I just weirdly dislike when information surfaces in my brain when I can't remember anything about myself. It . . . makes me feel dumb.

"Please help!"

I heard a woman's voice come from above. This time it wasn't the woman with Adrian. She didn't have an African accent or remotely close. Her voice sounded American. I spotted a staircase leading to where the cry must have originated. I scanned the area to make sure no one had the drop on me. I'd lost the woman and Adrian. There wasn't anywhere else to go but up. I'd come this far so turning back wasn't an option. My curiosity rose because I expected an unsanitary house full of women hostages and guards. I couldn't have been more wrong.

I took a deep breath, placed my hand on the rail of the steps, and looked up, trying to scan the second level. I took one precautionary step at a time, moving toward the unknown. I wondered if the woman who asked for help was alone. In any case, I would soon find out. Miss, are you alone? That's what I wanted to say, but those words could easily end my life. I reached the top of the steps and looked left and right down a very long corridor. Where are you, I thought. If I went room to room searching for the woman, I would surely run into trouble. One more time. I need to hear your voice for direction.

"Quit, bitch," I heard a male's voice followed by a slap.

Right on time. It wasn't her voice but useful. I now knew at least four people were in the house. Adrian, his hostage, the other woman, and her capturer. My mind said, turn around fool, and go back to the room. The same message I've been receiving since the beginning of this journey. And again, I ignored it.

I was the biggest thing in the hallway, and I crept along the wall as if I were invisible. Right end, roughly four doors down is where I heard the voice. I made it to the room safely.

"I need the fuckin' cure," I heard Adrian's voice.

"Why should I give it to you," I heard the other male. "You break into my home with nothing to offer."

"Please," I heard the woman. "Kill him! He is not to be trusted. He won't give you what you want."

Of course, the woman who was being kept hostage would try to convince Adrian to kill him. I slid in front of the door. I still didn't have a true count of the number of individuals on the other side, but I wanted to look. I tested the knob. Unlocked. I eased the knob clockwise and opened the door enough to capture a tiny peek of what was taking place.

"I said, quit," another slap.

"Enough," Adrian said sternly. "Where is the cure? Hand it over or I'll end your life. Your men are dead. There is no one here to protect you."

"This town is my protection," the man countered. "You won't make it out of this town without my consent, Black Water."

"You know my code name," Adrian said. "You must also know what I can do to a man, Casanova. That's correct, I know your code name as well."

Casanova, I thought. But, how? He didn't look anything like the guy in the ally who I knew for sure was dead.

"I know very well what you can do, assassin," the man assured Adrian.

I got a good look at the room. The woman Adrian took hostage was lying on the floor, sobbing as if she knew it was over for her. She betrayed Casanova by bringing Adrian to his domain. Adrian stood in front of the man. He wasn't very intimidating. A small African male around 5'8 at the most. Maybe 150 pounds soaking wet. The other woman was tied to a chair next to the man. She was an attractive brown skin woman with a nice body from what I could tell. She also had long dreadlocks, similar to my brother's hairstyle.

"You want the cure," Casanova continued. "I need you to kill the members of this woman's entourage. Her boyfriend came to this country with a small group of men. Kids, foolish enough to believe they can save his mother from the General. This request shouldn't be any trouble for a man with your skills. They're staying at the hotel. Do this for me and the cure is yours."

"Is this boyfriend of hers," Adrian walked toward the woman. "tall, well built with the same hairstyle, and goes by Kane?"

"That's correct, assassin," Casanova put his hand under his chin. "Where did you receive this information? Another man on your hit list I assume?"

A flurry of emotions hit in the same wave. My brother was at the hotel. Casanova knows something Adrian doesn't. Why would he lie? We're staying in the hotel and I didn't see anybody similar to the man I saw on the internet. The soldiers, prostitutes, and the woman with Adrian were the only personnel I saw moving about the establishment.

"It's none of your business," Adrian said. "I will kill the girl's boyfriend and the other members, but she has to come with me for insurance. After the job is complete. We'll swap the girl for the cure."

". . .," I watched Casanova ponder Adrian's offer. He stood and held out his hand. "This woman is my future wife. Protect her with your life. I need her returned safely or the deal is off."

"I will never marry you," the woman cried. "You sonova-"

Adrian didn't shake Casanova's hand. Instead, he swiftly grabbed the woman's jaw. "I like you better with your mouth shut, little one." I watched him free the woman from the chair. "Now, show me where Kane and his friends are hiding and I'll let you live. Worst case for you is marrying this asshole."

"Hey," Casanova said. "Watch what you say about me."

"Or what," Adrian didn't acknowledge Casanova. He kept his eyes on the woman.

" . . .," Casanova sighed.

"Meet me in front of the hotel in an hour," Adrian held the woman by her hair. "Don't be late."

The woman struggled with Adrian as he guided her by the hair. Suddenly, the woman's eyes locked with mine. I panicked, moved away from the door, and knocked over a vase sitting on a table. "Fuck," I couldn't catch it from falling to the floor. It shattered and created an undeniable intrusion alert.

"Someone's spying on us," I heard Casanova's shout.

I shot down the corridor, thinking about how I fucked up. It was clearly a rookie mistake. I heard all kinds of shouts and cries for help as I approached the staircase, but one voice, in particular, stood among the rest. It was the woman I locked eyes with. She'd shouted my name and it didn't sound like a cry for help. It sounded as if she was angered by my presence. Even her eyes read the same. I saw the pain in them. Something triggered that reaction. I couldn't have been visible. The door was barely cracked. If she could make out my eyes without me being fully exposed then there was something embedded in her memory of me. I wondered what that was. It couldn't have been good. Given the information I gained from Adrian and Casanova's conversation, the girl was Kane's girlfriend. She had to know of me through him. I pray there isn't any bad blood between us.

I stood at the top of the staircase and looked back down the corridor. Casanova was the first to leave the room. He stumbled into the hall as though he was learning to walk again. We even locked eyes before I descended the steps five at a time. Living room, dining room, kitchen, I was in front of the door to the basement. "What," the door was locked or jammed because I couldn't get the damn thing to open. I looked at the knob and there was a key entry. Safety lock, I thought. You could enter the house but couldn't leave without using the key. Casanova put in a safety precaution so the women couldn't escape.

" . . .," I groaned as I slammed my shoulder into the door. Pain hit it like a bullet. It didn't matter. It was the only way of escaping the house. I couldn't imagine the front door being unlocked for the public. I heard footsteps hustling through the living area. They're close, I thought. My shoulder felt as if it was about to explode as I barreled it at the door continuously until I fell through and down the steps, dragged behind the applied force. I quickly shot from the ground, ran toward the medieval door, and pulled it open.

The pathway down the tunnel appeared darker than before. I could have illuminated the way by using the lighter I found on the dead soldier up ahead, but it would have only slowed me down. It wouldn't keep flame at the speed I was moving. I had to remember not to trip over the rebel while running for my life.

Abel, the woman's voice rang out in my head as I thought about Adrian discovering the invader was me at the door. Suddenly, I ran over a soft lump that broke my perfect stride and nearly fell to the ground. The rebel. I stumbled a few paces but regained my balance and continued trucking, reaching the other end of the tunnel ten times faster than before. I slid to a stop in the small area and looked back for any signs of anyone in pursuit. I listened hard and didn't hear a sound nor did I see a light down the passage. Maybe Casanova took another route, I thought. They could cut off the other door entering the staircase from the hotel. I had to hurry so that wouldn't happen.

I took a deep breath and exhaled, thinking I was safe for now. I turned around and was taken by surprise. "Holy fuck!" I tried to react but it was too late. I instantly dropped to the ground after being struck in the head with the but of a gun. This was the end for me. I was gonna die in a dusty dungeon with no memory of who I was or my family. It was a sad feeling after getting so close to meeting my brother. If only I'd listened to Adrian and stayed put next to Jordan.

My last word was a grunt. I wished heroic words had come out as I fought for my life. However, I lay there sprawled out unable to move. I couldn't lift a finger to defend myself. As my vision began to fade, the last thing I saw was a patch over the left eye of the assailant.

37 – Several Hours Ago

"How was it," Noti watched Gina mutilate the Bazin. If they had met on other terms, she would have thought Gina had no table manners.

Gina stuffed the last piece of bread in her mouth and sucked her fingers afterward. The dish was incredible. She fell back in the chair and placed her hand on her stomach. "The food was good," she noticed Noti didn't lift a finger for the entire time. Her plate was dishwasher clean. "You're making me nervous."

"Why," Noti saw the way Gina eyed her plate. "Because I chose not to eat? Don't worry yourself. Nothing is wrong with the food. I wouldn't have gone through the trouble for your freedom. I had plenty."

Gina sighed. "I'm not dead yet. I suppose that's a good thing."

"Are you ready," Noti asked.

Gina gave you a look of curiosity.

217

"I'm taking you to meet the General," Noti stood from the seat. She couldn't believe a pretty girl like Gina would ever eat the way she put on display. When you're starving all bets are off the table, she thought.

"Why would the General want to meet me," Gina sat up straight. "I understand why you need me, but I'm curious to know what he wants."

"As I told you before," Noti said evenly. "I don't need you for anything. As for the General . . . well, convincing him that you're valuable to me is the only way you'll leave here alive. You were with Aayla. That makes you the enemy. I will have to do the same for my son. The both of you are way too deep."

"You are way too deep," Gina countered. "What is your reason for getting involved with the General?"

"You asked questions you know the answers to," Noti came back.

Gina raised her eyebrows. "And you are a very mischievous woman. I know you're hiding something. I don't think it's about the money for you. I saw the way you live. Your home is bigger than his building. Your nails are manicured and you have silky skin. Money doesn't impress you. A billion rolled off your tongue as if it was nothing. You're here because of your husband. You told me he's dead and still, you're here for him. You don't have to tell me why, just know I know it's not for money." Gina stood and walked to the door. "Let's go meet the General."

Noti smirked and turned around. "You're right. I'm not here for money. When this is done. You'll know my true intentions." Noti approached Gina and stared her in the eyes seriously. "You all will know." She put her hand on the knob and opened the door. "Come."

Gina followed Noti down the corridor. The facility had armed guards at every corner. The place gave her WWII vibes. They took a flight of stairs seven levels up. Her legs were worn by the time they reached the top. She thought about asking Noti why didn't they take the elevator but kept her mouth shut. They traveled down another long corridor until they reached a massive door with a gold plate display that read, *The General.*

Noti stopped before the door. "Keep your mouth shut. Only speak when you're spoken to."

Gina signaled with a nod.

Noti tapped on the door three times. "Abrafo."

Gina saw the man who aggressively handled her on two occasions. The first time she was captured by the General's men and when she was tossed into the cell. She held back her anger, trying to control herself from doing something she'd regret. She didn't have anything weapons to defend herself and there were several heavily armed guards along the way. She chose to hold off for now until the odds shifted in her favor.

Abrafo acknowledged Noti with a slight nod. "Queen." He kept his eyes on Noti as if Gina were invisible.

Noti nodded back and entered the massive office.

Gina followed behind Noti and sucked her teeth as she passed by Abrafo. It was loud enough for the soldier to hear. The disrespect was the same. She understood that she wasn't worth a grain of rice to them. There wasn't a man alive who would openly put her behind their feet without her presence being acknowledged. She kept her eyes forward with extreme confidence that no harm would come to her. She made it to the office alive. That was enough assurance for her.

The General faced the window as the women entered his domain. Every now and again, he'd watch birds fly and wondered what life would be like if he were as free as them. He saw Noti's reflection as she entered the room. "Queen Noti," his strong accent carried the room.

Noti stopped at the head of the desk. "General," she greeted pleasantly.

"Do you have the African Black Diamond," the General got right down to business.

"No, General," she knew he would get to the point if she requested a meeting. He valued his time more than anyone she'd ever met. That was one thing she respected about him. "It's been less than twenty-four hours since I've arrived. I need one more day and it will be in your hands."

The General signed and turned to their attention. "Is she the one?"

"Yes," Noti answered. "The girl will lead us to the diamond. I need her alive to fulfill my promise. Please spare her life, General."

The General eyed the small girl Noti brought before him. "What is your name girl?"

"Gina," she kindly replied with everything she had inside, trying not to piss the General off. She didn't come this far just to come this far.

"Umph," he turned his attention back to Noti. "I hope she won't disappoint me like the FBI agent you recommended for the diamond heist. I lost some of my best soldiers that day. Her failer is your life."

"I apologize for Jordan's mishap," Noti answered gracefully. "I was unaware he would involve my sons and his insanity. I assume you. The girl is different."

"What is evident about her," the General asked.

Gina couldn't believe what she'd heard spill from Noti's mouth. The Planner was revealed to the world as FBI agent Jordan. He was all over the news as the mastermind behind the museum heist. The same individual who hired Abel to steal it. Noti was the link between The General and Jordan and the true mastermind. Before she thought too hard about it. She needed to prove her worth to the General. She raised her left wrist, showing off the watch given to her by Snake. "Let me show you what true advanced technology can do."

38 – KANE

"Kim," I shouted her name multiple times, hoping she would appear. I stood in the middle of the road, lost. "Kim . . .! Baby, please, if you can hear me make a sound so I can find you!" I dropped to my knees and put my face in my hands. My emotions were running wild. I lost her, I thought. I fuckin' lost her.

"Kane," I felt a hand on my shoulder.

"She's gone, man," I looked up at Bear with tears in my eyes. "I don't know what to do. I checked everywhere." I began explaining what happened. "I woke up to the shower running and she didn't answer when I knocked on the door. She wasn't in there. I didn't hear a thing when I was asleep. Why would she leave the room with the shower running? I told her I would protect her. It's all my fault." I looked down at the ground. "I fucked up, Bear."

"Get up, big dawg," Bear said calmly. "Don't let these mafuckas see you like this."

Bear helped me get up from the ground. "What am I gonna do without her?"

222

"We found someone I think can help," he said.

"Who," I replied with a sense of hope. "Tell me."

"You need to see for yourself," he said. "Come on. He's in our room."

I led the way, eager to see who Bear was referring to. Who could this person be? Did they see Kim leave the room? I had so many questions I didn't know what to ask first. Any piece of information would be valuable. I beat Bear to the room they were staying in and tried to open the door. Fuck, I didn't have a key so I knocked. "Open up, it's me." I banged on the door.

"I got it," Bear approached the door and opened it with his keycard. He held the door slightly open and turned to me with a serious look in his eyes. "Whatever you do . . . don't fuckin' lose it. You're gonna want to hear what he has to say."

"Ok," I answered ready to burst through the door.

Bear opened the door, walked inside, and held it open for me.

I walked inside cautiously as if I was being set up by my friend. Bear's demeanor was much different than normal. Something was going on. I stood by the door and scanned the room. I spotted Smoke leaning against the dresser with a stressful facial expression. Big Bruce stood by the window and he didn't look too good either. Doo-Rag stood in the middle of the room in front of someone sitting in a chair. His back was turned to me. I walked over and kindly moved him to the side.

Mufucka, I thought. I swiftly removed my gun from my back waist and pressed it against Abel's forehead. "I fuckin' know it," I growled.

"Don't do it," Smoke's voice rang out unexpectedly. "He knows where to find sis."

I didn't bother to look at Smoke and kept my eyes on Abel. His hands were tied behind the chair and his head was down. He looked exhausted. I was too angry to respond to Smoke.

"I found him in the basement," Doo-Rag spoke up. "Smoke told us what happened to Kim. We went searching for her down there. It was the obvious place to look. There was a passage leading to barrels of fresh water in the basement of a house. That was as far as we got. Another door inside the basement was torn down and we didn't want to proceed. He was running for his life. Too dangerous. He won't speak unless it's with you." Doo-Rag stepped back and gave me the floor. "Do as you must. He's yours."

I placed the barrel of the gun under Abel's chin and lifted his head. He could barely open his eyes. I was right the whole time. Abel was the man fighting in the ally. If I had acted then maybe Kim wouldn't have gone missing. I wanted to pull the trigger so badly that the nerves in my hand caused the weapon to shake. A ton of things surface in my mind. How my life changed after Abel murdered his teacher. Murdering our father in cold blood, and what he did to Kim. "Where is she?"

"Brother," Abel said tiredly.

"I'm not your fuckin' brother," I growled. "Where the fuck is Kim?"

"Please," his eyes opened and closed a few times as if he was drinking all night. "I need you to listen to me. I'm not who you think I am."

"Answer the fuckin' question," I pressed his head back with the gun.

"I need to tell you what happened first," Abel looked me in the eyes.

"What did you do to her," I asked angrily. "If you touched her!"

"I didn't do anything to her," Abel said. "Just listen to what I have to say."

I sighed. "Go ahead."

"I . . .," Abel stammered. "I . . . lost . . . I lost my memory."

"You have to be a stupid mufucka if you expect me to believe that bullshit," I looked around the room in shock that he would even try a lie of such idiocy. "Y'all hear this guy?"

"Same shit he told us," Bear said with a shrug.

Even though Smoke and I were on bad terms I looked at him for assurance. He gestured with his hands and shook his head.

"You're the smartest person I've ever known," I turned back to Abel. "If this is how you expect to stay alive by lying to me about losing your memory then you're a fool. I can't believe that's what you came up with. I'll give you one more chance to tell me where I can find Kim. If I don't hear directions come from your mouth, you're brains will be on the back wall."

"I don't expect you to believe me," Abel continued. "Jordan told me everything I did to you."

"You're working with him," I roared in his face.

"Listen to me," Abel snapped. "I woke up after the accident and he was standing over me with Adrian."

"That fuck boy," I heard Smoke in the background.

"That's how I lost my memory," he continued. "Jordan was about to kill me until Adrian somehow performed a lie detector test on me. They want to use me to get to you and our mother."

"Don't you fuckin' dare say our mother," I growled. "Not after you murdered our father!" I felt my heartbeat kick into high gear. It felt like I was having a heart attack. My chest heaved uncontrollably. I placed my hand over my chest, feeling like I was about to faint.

"You good," I heard Bruce. "You might want to take a seat. You look like you're about to pass out."

"I'm straight," I said, holding the back of my hand on my forehead.

"Take a seat," Bear slid the desk chair behind me.

I sat down and scooted close to Abel until we were face to face. I closed my eyes and took a deep breath and when I opened them I saw tears streaming down Abel's face.

"I . . .," Abel choked on his words. "I . . . murdered our father?"

I wanted to slap the shit out of him for trying me, but his facial expression held me at bay. I can't remember the last time I saw him cry. It blew my mind. Something was off and I took a moment to stare deep into his eyes. Shockingly, he appeared to be . . . heartbroken.

39 – ABEL

"I . . . murdered our father," I stared back at my brother with teary eyes. Why would he say something so hurtful? I would never commit a crime of that magnitude. Why punish me for something I didn't . . . my brother's stare broke my train of thought. His eyes remained on me and I didn't see them blink. I figured someone in the game caught up to my father and took him out. Jordan claimed that my father was an arms dealer. It made sense if that's what happened to him.

"Don't look so sad," I heard a change in Kane's voice. He no longer spoke in an angry tone. It was a bit more settled. "You're a monster, Abel Simmons. I went to jail for a murder you committed."

The teacher, I thought. But . . .

"From there. Our father," Kane had a terrifying look in his eyes as if he was holding back on his promise to put my brains on the wall. "Not only are you a murderer, but a rapist."

"K . . . Kim," I thought about how she looked at me when we locked eyes in the house. If eyes could commit murder I'd be dead. That's the look she gave me.

228

"Kim," Kane repeated evenly. "I'll never forgive you for what you have done to me and for destroying our family. You deserve everything that comes to you. There is nothing you can say or do to stop me from taking your life. Today will be your last day on earth. The best thing you can do if there's a bit of hope to save your soul, is to tell me where I can find Kim."

I dropped my head down in shame. I couldn't look my brother in the eyes for what I did to him and our family. I heard anger and the pain in his voice. It was the truth and there was no way around it. I did what he said I'd done. I am a monster. "I understand and thank you for listening. Jordan is in room 2B. He's sick and close to dying. He drank the water at the bar and Adrian sat out to find Casanova to get the cure."

"Bullshit," Smoke broke in. "It's a setup."

"It's not," I lifted my head. "Casanova poisoned the water. That's how he separates the women from their partners. He dumps the men in a wall and traffick the women, selling them on the black market to the highest bidder."

"The rebels dump the bodies of the General's men in the lake," Kane replied. "That's how the water got polluted, poisoned, whatever you want to call it. They call it –"

"Blood Lake," I interrupted.

"You know which doesn't matter," Kane replied.

"Tell me," I said. "Have you seen a lake anywhere around here?" I saw the look on his face, confirming he hadn't. "It matters because Casanova took Kim."

Kane jumped out of his seat. "Where is he!"

"He doesn't have her," I said. "The only way you will get her back is to go to room 2B and capture Jordan. I followed Adrian and the woman who was at the front desk. The pathway through the basement led to a house where Casanova imprisoned the women. That's where I saw Kim. Before I was spotted, I overheard Casanova and Adrian agreeing to exchange the cure for your death. If Adrian successfully kills you and the others. Casanova will give him what he wants. Adrian took Kim for assurance."

"What do you want to do," the big guy Kane called Bear spoke up.

"Take Bruce, and Doo-Rag and hit 2B," Kane told him. "Be careful. If he's in there like he said. Move him to the room with the little soldiers and Aasir. If Jordan is a problem, you know what to do. Report back to me immediately."

"Done," Bear said and left with the two men.

"If you're lying to me," Kane stood over me. "You're dead."

"I want you to know," I started. "I'm truly sorry for the things I've done. You don't have to believe a word from my mouth or that I lost my memory. It seems there is no way to repair our relationship. I only wish I had been a different man. I hope the information helps you on your journey. Please . . . save your woman, our mother, and you and your friends leave this place for good. I don't deserve to live. You can kill me." I lowered my head and seconds later I felt Kane press the gun to the back of my skull.

Suddenly, I heard the other guy speak up. "Wait. What if he's telling the truth? Do you really want to kill him if he doesn't recall any of the shit he's done?"

Kane removed the gun from my head and sat in the chair in front of me. He sighed before speaking. "What if he's telling the truth." He paused and eyed me. "Smoke, do you actually think he'll tell me the truth?"

"If the gang finds Jordan," Smoke walked over and put his hand on Kane's shoulder. "Then, I would believe so. You're my dawg, fuck what happened earlier. We don't even need to speak on it. I wouldn't steer you wrong. I can feel it. I mean, look at him. He has nothing to lose. Dude is fucked up, and tied to a chair. Jordan sure as hell wouldn't risk his life for him. Adrian wouldn't and we have his boys in the other room. Them niggas soft. Everything he told you adds up. Doo-Rag finds him in the basement and Kim is missing. Where else could she have gone? Even if he's lying, he's defeated. You know I'm the last nigga who would spare him after what he did to sis."

At that very moment, I saw compassion in my brother's eyes. "Right, but there isn't a have we can tell if he lost his memory. It's not like I can ask him a question that only we would know."

"There isn't a question you could ask," I told him. "However, there is one thing I would like to know if you don't mind answering."

"What is that," Kane said.

"I saw a family picture of us on the internet," I smiled, thinking about how silly it sounded referring to a family photo of us under the circumstances. "After Jordan told me I had a brother. I wanted to know what you looked like. Come to find out, you and our father look the same. Even have the same hairstyle. Why didn't I have the same style?"

"That's your question," Smoke said amazed. "Wow, this guy."

"Humph," Kane smirked. "Out of all the questions you could have asked. You chose that one."

"Yes," I assured them. "I want to know why I don't look like our father."

"Ok," Kane said. "You shaved your head bald when you were a child. You cut a spot on the top of your head preventing your hair from growing. You've been rocking a baldy ever since. You attempted to cut my shit off too but our mother caught you. You two were very close."

"And you were close to our father," I asked.

Kane shrugged.

"That would be the reason I didn't feel anything for him when I saw his photo," I said. "Why is that?"

"That's how it was, dude," he said exasperated. "Listen, you know all this. Stop acting like a peanut head."

I smiled. "Peanut head, huh? You're right, and I'm supposed to be the smart one. How in the hell did I get into Yale."

Kane stood, "Maybe he did lose his memory."

"What makes you say that now," Smoke asked.

"I called him a Peanut head and he didn't even flinch," Kane kept his eyes on me.

"Why would I –"

"That's right . . .," Smoke said excitedly and looked at me. "You used to get mad as fuck when Kane called you that when you went bald so you started calling him a Knucklehead. That shit infuriated you." Smoke looked at Kane. "Damn, that was a smart move. You knew he would react if he hadn't lost his memory. Fuckin' genius, nigga. Bravo?" He clapped his hands. "Bra-fuckin'-vo, my guy."

"It's a small step," Kane said. "Still doesn't mean anything until we find out if he was telling the truth."

Suddenly, the door burst open. It was the big guy, Bear. "We have Jordan. He told us the truth."

40 – KANE

"Watch'em," I told Smoke.

"Yep," Smoke said.

I rushed out of the room with Bear.

The room was across the hall. Bear inserted the keycard into the door. "He's not all there, dawg," he said before opening it.

I nodded at him before entering the room. It didn't matter to me if The Planner was all there or not. He tried to kill me and my friends on multiple occasions. Now that he's in a vulnerable state shouldn't affect a change in outcome. This is war. There can only be one victor. He would do what's needed if it was me. There are no rules in this game.

I crossed the threshold and spotted Jordan lying on his stomach sprawled out on the bed. He wasn't moving. Bear and Bruce didn't bother to prop him up straight or sit him in a chair. Abel's boys were standing next to the bed. They were checking the time on their watches as if they had somewhere to be. I found it odd the watches were the same. Big Bruce was sitting in the chair with his legs crossed and his head back. I could tell he was exhausted from what's been going on for the past few days. I walked over to the bed. "Is he asleep or dead?"

"He's sick as fuck," Bear replied. "The water did a number on him. I'm glad Aasir put us on game."

"Right," I said trying to figure out my next move.

"Speaking of Aasir," Bear continued. "Where is he? I haven't seen him in a hot minute."

"Don't know," I muttered, keeping my eyes on Jordan.

Bear walked over and stood next to me. "What do you wanna do with him?"

"If Adrian does have Kim," I said. "We can trade him for her."

"What if he dies before we get the chance," Bear asked.

"We better find Adrian fast before that happens," I told him while grabbing Jordan's right leg. "Help me flip him over. I wanna see his face."

Bear slid his massive paws under Jordan's shoulder and abdomen. "Ready."

I nodded and we flipped Jordon onto his back. "My God," I said after seeing his face. Not only was it turning purple but one side of his face was destroyed. The wrapping around his head had begun to unravel. It was barely together. Kim got him good with the rocket launcher. I'd wish she killed him but here we are, hoping he would survive long enough to swap for her.

"I don't know what I would do if I looked like that," Bear said. "He an't fuckin' nothing but his hand."

I sighed. "Money is the new look, big dawg."

"Straight up," Bruce chimed in. "Money will change a hoe's perspective."

"It doesn't seem that way," Surprisingly, it was Snake who spoke up. "The girls at our school don't seem to care."

"That's because the girls at your school are stuck up and rich," I said. "They don't know any better. Their opinion will change when they hit the wall."

"True dat," Bear added. "Ya'll fuckin' with the wrong breed. You can find a bad bitch who is less fortunate by dating down." Bear sighed. "And y'all supposed to be smart. Fuckin' virgins."

Bruce laughed. "Rich niggas and don't get any pussy."

"Um . . .," Bam began to speak. "I'm mixed."

"Shut the fuck up," Bear said. "I'm mixed. Nigga you're black."

"A'ight," I held up my hand. "Let's focus."

"That's him," I heard Snake whisper.

"Who," Bam whispered back.

"The Planner," he said. "The guy who hired us to steal the diamond."

"Hey, smart guy," I looked at Snake.

"Yes," he answered with a worried look in his eyes.

"I need some advice," I said seriously.

"Of course," he replied. "I'm happy to help."

"I'm in a complex situation," I began. "My girlfriend was kidnapped by his brother." I pointed to Jordan. "Who set up a deal for our lives." I pointed at everyone in the room, including them. Their eyes grew to the size of eggs.

"This can't be good," Bam muttered.

"Believe me," I continued. "It's not good. Adrian is his name and he's an assassin. He made a deal with a man who goes by Casonava. When we all are dead, Casanova will hand over a cure to save his life and will force my girl's hand in marriage."

I saw Snake shaking his head.

"Any ideas," I asked.

Snake sighed. "If Abel were here. He would know what to do."

"Ok," I smirked, looking at their confused faces. "Let's find out what he thinks."

41 – ABEL

"My bad," Smoke said after shutting the bathroom door. "Had to drain the weasel." He sat in the chair Kane was previously in right in front of me. He sighed before speaking. "So, where were we?"

I looked Smoke in the eyes. The man I assume to be Kane's most trusted ally and friend. His eyes told me there was tension between us. "Did I do something to anger you?"

"Not to me," Smoke responded while keeping his eyes locked on mine.

He left it there and stayed quiet as if he wanted me to guess what I'd done. "Do . . . you want to tell me what happened?"

"Memory loss," Smoke sighed. "right?"

I nodded. "Yes." I couldn't remember anything about Smoke. I assume there was never a time we were friends. Brothers usually don't befriend the same people due to different personalities. "Whatever it is, I'm sorry."

He smirked. "You're sorry, huh?" He stood and looked down at me. "As a man of my word. I can't accept your apology."

"I understand," I answered. "However you like to judge me. I truly want to help my brother get back Kim."

"Keep her name out of your fuckin' mouth," Smoke walked behind me. Suddenly, I felt the binds loosen. "Get up."

"You're doing this because of her," I asked as my hands dropped free. Blood began to flow in my arms and wrists. Unbelievable, I thought. He trusted me enough to set me free while alone. "What . . . I did to her affected you." I remained seated as I watched him walk to the table.

"Honestly," he revealed a weapon and ejected the clip. He looked it over and set the gun and clip on the table. "I don't give a damn if you lost your memory or if you're lying about it." He turned around and faced me. I stared into the eyes of a demon. "This is about respect, honor, and loyalty. Regardless of our circumstances. You feel me."

I held up my hands to show I wasn't a threat. He was clearly acting on emotion.

"Put your fuckin' dukes up," Smoke took a fighting stance.

"I don't want to fight," I kept my hands where he could see them. "We're wasting time. We could be out there looking for Adrian."

"Stop pretending you care, homeboy," Smoke growled at me. "It's just me in here. Drop the act. You know what it is."

"It's not an act," I said frustrated. "Kim needs our help."

"What did I say about keeping her name out of your mouth," Smoke roared and rushed at me. He wrapped his arms around my waist and speared me into the chair.

"Ah," I groaned falling over the chair onto the ground. His weight came down on me and forced the edge of the seat into my backbone. A sharp pain manifest throughout my spine. I had enough strength to toss him off of me. I stood at least five inches taller and outweighed him by at least fifty pounds and yet, his emotions told him to disregard our differences.

I remained on the floor and reached for my back as Smoke hopped onto his feet. He kicked me in the side and stomped on my head several times. My body retracted into a fetal position and I covered my head with my arms. The room became a blur and the only thing I could see was the Air Jordan symbol on the bottom of his shoe.

"Ah," I cried after being struck by the chair I was sitting in. Smoke was on a rampage.

"Get your pussy ass up," I heard him growl.

"Please stop," my right palm was on the ground and I was hunched over on one knee. "Ah!" Smoke didn't listen to my plea and broke the chair over my back, forcing me to the floor. I lay on my stomach unable to move. I had to dig deep and pick myself up. I couldn't let him beat me to death. No matter how hard I try, I wouldn't convince Smoke to stop. His manhood was on the line.

"You might not remember a thing," Smoke paused his assault on me. "But you will remember this ass whipping on everything I love, nigga."

I got back to a knee which wasn't easy. I held up my hand trying to defend myself. I didn't know what he would do next. Smoke struck me in the face with a closed fist. It wasn't powerful enough to drop me. I kept my arm out trying to determine where the next shot would come from. I moved my arm around, shielding my face from the next shot.

"This is for sis," Smoke connected with another shot. This time it hit the opposite side of my face. It could have been that I was delirious, but it sounded like he was crying. People tend to cry when something deeply affects them emotionally and even overcoming that obstacle hurts.

"Please stop," I tried again to stop the assault as I finally stood on my feet. I tasted the blood from my nose in my mouth. My ribs were in pain and my head hurt like hell. Smoke was right. I would remember this ass whipping. The room slowly became clear. My blurry vision was gone. I saw Smoke standing by the table and after I heard a click. I knew it was one. He was about to use the weapon to kill me.

"It's over nigga," by the time Smoke turned around it was too late.

He was surprised to see I was in his face. He tried to aim the gun and I grabbed it, forcing his arm toward the ceiling as a shot rang out. I swiftly punched him in the face with my free hand. I put everything I had into it, summoning enough strength to drop him.

"Fuck," he cried down on one knee. He swiftly looked at me ready to attack, but the weapon had him frozen. "Do it, nigga. End this shit."

I aimed the gun at his head. I could put a bullet in his skull and no one would know he was dead until his body was discovered because the weapon was equipped with a suppressor. I looked into his bloodshot eyes and knew he wasn't afraid of death. I have to kill this man or somewhere down the line when we cross paths again, he'll attempt to kill me. There was nothing I could do to fix his emotional state. His behavior wouldn't change toward me regardless of how hard he tried. It would take a miracle for him to forgive what I had done to Kim. The woman he called his sister. If our roles were changed, I would more than likely act the same. This had to be done. I couldn't think of any other option that would save one of us from a tragic death. "I wish you could find it in your heart to forgive me but that doesn't seem likely. I have to find Adrian and put an end to this. I'm sorry, but I have to do this." I looked into Smoke's eyes like a man before emptying the clip. I dropped the gun on the floor next to him and left the room in search of Adrian.

42 – We're Friends TOO

"You're a black sonovabitch," Johnny and three of his had me pinned against my locker.

"What kind of name is Abel anyway," Billy said over Johnny's shoulder. "You're new name is Blacky."

The boys laughed.

"Blacky," Eddie repeated. "That's a good one, Billy."

"You guys are idiots," I told them while struggling to get free. "and racist."

"Teach him a lesson for calling us idiots, Johnny," Charley suggested.

"Yeah, show'em who's boss, Johnny," Billy egged Johnny. "Kick his ass."

"We're idiots, huh, smart guy," Johnny gripped the collar of my shirt with one hand and rubbed my bald head with the other. Purposefully trying to embarrass me.

"Ah," I grunted after Johnny punched me in the stomach. The gang of four only came after the smart kids. Not only that, I'm a freshman taking honor classes. The boys were a bunch of dumb Juniors who should have graduated by now. Instead of hitting the books, they choose to terrorize the intelligent. I couldn't take any more beatings from them. Today would be the day I stand up to Johnny and his crew.

"Fuck," Johnny release me and fell to the ground holding his crotch.

The boys stood there with confused faces.

I took off running after kicking Johnny in the balls.

I heard Johnny shout from behind, *kill 'em!*

It was the end of the day and there wasn't a teacher in site. I looked through the windows of the classroom doors frantically as I ran by. Every door I tried was locked. I had to get somewhere safe where the boys couldn't find me, I thought. Suddenly, a sign of hope presented itself. I saw my math teacher up ahead walk into his classroom. He could get the boys off my back.

I slid to a stop in front of the door and tried to open it. "Mr. Ingram," I shouted. He'd locked the door. "Mr. Ingram! Please open the door!"

Mr. Ingram turned around and waved me off and continued toward his desk.

I shouted again. "Mr. Ingram, I need your help!" He ignored me. I spotted a student in the room, standing by Mr. Ingram's desk. It was Kelly, the first girl I ever had a crush on. I noticed she had tears in her eyes. "Please! Johnny is trying to kill me!"

Mr. Ingram casually walked to the door and pulled down the curtain on the window.

At the moment, I knew he wouldn't be any help. He never liked me. He thought I was too smart for my own good. That's probably why I never got an A+ in his class. "I won't forget this!" I shouted angrily.

I stepped back from the door. I heard Johnny and his crew fast approaching. With nowhere to hide, I made a horrible decision and ran into the boys' restroom. I chose the stall on the far end and locked myself inside. My heart raced and my hands wouldn't stop shaking. I wish I had a bodyguard which was a ridiculous thing to ask for but kids who get bullied, need someone. The little friends I have are weak and I would only put them in harm's way in a fight.

I sat on the toilet and tried to stop my knees from clapping. I was scared the boys would find me. Suddenly, the door burst open. I held my breath for dear life as I heard Johnny's voice.

"Blacky," he said, sarcastically. "I knew you're in here hiding like a coon."

". . .," I tried to remain as quiet as possible.

"Come out, come out, wherever you are," Johnny continued to taunt me. He took pride in people being afraid of him.

Get it together Abel, I told myself. They're going to find you so, go out there and stand up for yourself. Fight like a man and stop being a chicken. This is one of the only times I wished Kane were here to help.

We're twins but he's bigger and stronger than me. Maybe because he chose to play sports and I chose to read. Damnit, I thought.

"Hey Blacky," Billy spoke up. "Are you hiding in the last stall?"

They know where I am. Ok, then. I made a decision and came out of the stall. "Fuck you guys. Bring it!" I put my hands up and got in a fighting stance. It was the same stance Bruce Lee took in The Last Dragon. I didn't know how to fight, but they didn't know that. My plan was to trick them into believing I knew martial arts.

"Look at him," Johnny laughed. "What are you gonna do? Take us all on like you're some kind of Karate expert?"

"He's bluffing," Eddie suggested. "He doesn't know how to fight?"

I stared the boys down, putting on the most menacing face I could muster. "Why don't you be the first to find out." I held my palm out flat and gestured for him to come get some.

Surprisingly, Eddie rushed over and caught a punch to the face. "Fuck," he backed off.

Charely came storming in and I kicked him in the stomach. He fell to the ground, "It hurts."

I looked at my hands in shock. "Fuck, I can fight."

"You're dead," Johnny growled and said to Billy. "Get'em."

Billy had a concerned tone. "You get'em first."

"What," Johnny replied. "Are you a chicken shit?"

"Same time then," Billy said.

I was too busy looking at my hands in amazement after taking down two boys. I couldn't believe it. That was a mistake on my part. The boys rushed at me simultaneously. They took me down and pounded on my body til I could no longer block their blows.

"How do you like that, Blacky," I heard Johnny.

It felt like punches and kicks were raining down on me from every direction until . . . it stopped.

"Get the fuck off my dawg," I heard a familiar voice. Someone was here to save me. I couldn't immediately make out the hero. I gained the strength to get back on my feet. Blood spilled from my nose and I knew I had a busted lip. I shook it off and took a fighting stance but there wasn't no one to fight.

"You good," Smoke asked.

"Wha," I couldn't believe who was standing in front of me. Smoke had annihilated Johnny and his crew.

Eddie was lying on his back, Charley had the garbage can over his head, Billy was out cold under the sink, and Johnny's head was in the toilet.

"Fuckin' pussies," Smoke spat on Eddie.

"How did you know," I asked.

"I saw them chasing after you," Smoke said. "I couldn't help then because I had five minutes left of detention. I couldn't leave that shit. They would've given me another day, you feel me."

I picked up my bag and strapped it around my shoulders. "Where's Kane?"

"Track field," he said.

"Oh, right," I replied. "Hey, don't tell him. I don't want to be looked at as a . . . pussy."

"You're good, dawg," he replied. "I won't say a thing and if you don't want your brother's help, you need to take some self-defense classes or some shit. You can't be running around getting your ass kicked for free."

"You're right, I do need to learn how to defend myself," I said. "Thank you."

Smoke walked toward the door, "No problem."

Just when he was about to leave I stopped him. "Hey, Smoke."

He turned around and held the door open. "Whaddup?"

"Why did you help me," I asked curiously.

He smirked and shook his head. "Because we're friends too."

I watched Smoke leave the restroom. "We're friends too."

43 – ABEL

I rushed out of the door, heading back to 2B. I had to verify that Kane left the room. Adrian would kill him for sure. Hopefully, Adrian had other plans. I moved curiously through the halls, praying not to run into Kane or the others. I couldn't let them put a hold on what I had to do. Adrian had to be stopped. Not only for Kim but for my mother's sake. She was on Jordan's hit list. Both men had to be dealt with.

I made it to the room without a problem. The door was cracked open. I pushed through, thankful the bomb had been removed. I didn't see or hear anyone. That gave me a sign of relief. Kane was gone and Adrian hadn't returned to the room. The man with the patch over his eye took my weapon when I was captured. I needed a new one. Adrian placed Jordan's gun inside the dresser after he'd gotten sick. I walked over and pulled back the drawer, relieved it was still there. "Yes," I muttered, setting my eyes on it. Gun, clip, all good. I loaded a bullet into the chamber and holstered the weapon. I had everything I needed to go after Adrian.

I left the room, thinking about where to look first. Adrian would need to go somewhere open but safe. Kane has a crew and Adrian is without Jordan. However, Adrian is a deadly assassin so how would an assassin gain the advantage? He must have a secure place to hide the hostage. Where would he take Kim while entertaining a fight to the death? Three places came to mind. This first would be somewhere in the hotel. He could have hidden her in another room or taken her to the rooftop. He wouldn't risk running into Kane or an occupied room.

I made my way down the hall in a hurry, rushing because Kane would be looking for me after they found Smoke. I opened the doorway to the staircase leading to the basement. The second place I figured Adrian would hold Kim was the mansion. Since I didn't know where the house was exactly located, I decided to head back the way I came. After Kim sounded the alarm, Adrian might've had a change of plans. He could have set up to lead Kane there instead of leaving the mansion. It would be the obvious revision. It was a safe place to hide Kim and big enough to take on each of the men. They didn't know the layout and Adrian could easily pick them off one by one. They would enter an unknown space, giving Adrian the advantage. Casanova could also aid the assassin with men to even the odds.

I ran down the stairs and stopped before the tunnel. It was still dark as if somehow Casanova would have left the light on for me. I sighed and bolted down the tunnel trying not to waste time. I thought about Casanova securing the pathway with men, but a guy like him wouldn't waste any resources without proper cause. They would want Kane to enter the mansion.

I pushed through the historic door and entered the basement at the other end of the tunnel. It was the same scene as before. Barrels of water were the only thing in sight. So far so good, I thought, entering the domain. I expected the place to be in an uproar. It was ultra quiet and I thought my ears had deceived me. There had to be someone, somewhere in the house.

I crept through the kitchen into the living room. Everything appeared normal after taking a brief scan of the area. I stopped in front of the stairs and looked up, listening for any sounds of movement. It crossed my mind before entering that it could be a trap for my brother. Instead of capturing him, they'd get me. Would the mouse take the cheese if he knew it was a trap? One foot in front of the other, I made it to the top without a sound. Down the hall to my right was clear. Casanova's room was on the left side. His room was where I saw Kim. That's where the search began. As I made my way down the hall, I couldn't help looking over my shoulder. Every step I took, I thought Adrian would jump out of nowhere and kill me. Even though I had a gun, I felt it wasn't enough to stop him. The weapon would jam with the kind of luck I've had lately.

I took a deep breath and exhaled, standing before Casanova's bedroom door. I held the gun with two hands like a policeman, making sure it was secure. I was scared to the point it could slip out of my hands. Stop being a coward and go inside. Kim needs your help. That's what I told myself before placing the tip of my boot on the door and cautiously pushing it open. The nose of the gun led the way inside. If someone was in there. The chrome triangular tip would be the first thing they'd see. They might as well fire at the door. It was a better option than sticking my head inside and getting it blown off.

I stepped past the threshold and it was satisfying nowhere was inside to confront me. Unfortunately, neither was Kim. Casanova, Adrian, Kim, and the woman from the desk were all gone. It was as if no one was here an hour ago. Why is it so quiet, I thought. Where could they have gone?

". . .," I swiftly turned around after hearing a woman murmur.

Kim, I thought. The voice didn't come from inside the room. However, it did sound awfully close. I stood in the middle of the room with the gun aimed at the door, wishing Casanova or Adrian would poke their head through. I held my ground for several seconds before taking fractional steps toward the door. I wanted to call out to Kim but couldn't risk exposing myself. I did want to make it out alive.

With the gun leading the way, I stepped into the hallway. The soft cries continued. They were coming from the room across the hall to the left, heading back toward the stairs. I got to the door in a hurry, not wanting to waste time. I put my hand on the knob and turned. Surprinelgy, it opened. I couldn't believe my eyes. There were four people in the room and not the people I thought to be.

"Please," the woman from the desk cried. "Don't kill us."

"I . . .," I stammered, unable to speak. The women were hugging each other in the middle of the room as if it were their last time on earth. I laid my eyes on a girl whom I had mistaken for a woman. She couldn't have been any older than fifteen if my mind served me correctly.

"I don't want to die," the small girl said.

"Don't take my sisters," the woman from the desk asked. "Here," she held out her hand. "You can take back the diamonds. Just leave us be. I beg you."

"These . . . are your sisters," I asked, looking them over. I took my eyes off them for a moment to scan the surroundings. Casanova or Adrian would have been on my ass by now.

"Yes," she said with tears in her eyes. "They came here with me and my husband. Casanova took them from me."

"You're hostages," I asked.

"Yes," she cried. "I thought he sold them on the black market, but he kept them for himself. I found them after Casanova left with the man and woman."

"Why haven't you escaped," I asked. "Leave this place while you can."

"We cannot," she said. "They are not free." She pointed to their ankles.

My eyes traveled downward. "Shackles," I muttered. I thought about walking them out of the house but that would be too dangerous. It was the only option that came to mind. I approached and crouched near the woman and the youngest shrieked backwards. "It's ok. You don't have to be afraid. I'm not going to harm you." She nodded and I examined the chains around their ankles. The three sisters were linked by a two-foot chain and shackle. They had room to walk but not run.

"He will kill us if we try to escape," I heard one of the sisters.

"Do you know where he keeps the key," I asked. It was a long shot but just maybe . . . they knew.

"The mean man with two gold teeth and a scar on his cheek," the girl answered. "He is the one who brought us here with the rest of the women. He's Casanova's brother."

"The man with the gold teeth and scar . . .," I muttered, thinking about the man I bumped into in the pissy staircase whom I killed in the alley. Casanova must have given him the dog tags. I dug in my pocket and pulled out the set of keys. One of them resembled a key for a lock.

The girl's eyes lit up. "That's the key!"

"Shh . . .," The woman from the desk shushed her sister.

I tried the key and the first of three shackles dropped to the floor. I continued freeing the woman and when I was done, they gave me the most caring group hug I'd ever felt in my life. They were overjoyed.

"Take them," I handed the woman from the desk the keys. "This one goes to one of the Jeeps in front of the hotel. Head back through the tunnel, it's clear. No one will see you. Don't stop for anyone or anything."

The women cried after embracing me a second time.

"Take the diamonds for freeing us," the woman held them out to me.

"Keep them," I told her. "Use them to start a new life."

"Thank you," she said and put them back in her pocket. "What is your name?"

"Abel," I told her.

"We will never forget you, Abel," she said. "You are a great man. I wish there was a way to repay you."

"Maybe there is a way you can help," I said. "Do you know where Casanova or the man took the woman? She is a friend of mine and I wish to save her life."

"Yes," she replied. "They took her to the bar. I heard them mention it when we were in Casanova's room. They want to kill the man who looks like you. I saw him in the hotel with the woman."

I pulled out the tube with the green substance. "Do you know what this is?"

"Yes," the woman from the desk said. "Medicine for the bad water."

"Thank you," I said after she clarified the third location I had in mind. "You don't know how much this means to me. Please, leave now. Take the pathway through the basement and remember what I said. I will take the front door as a distraction."

They all thanked me again and we left the room together.

We got to the bottom of the staircase. I watched them approach the basement door. The youngest turned to me before entering. "Be safe on your journey. God is with you, Abel." She smiled and vanished before my eyes.

I sat there with tears in my eyes. I don't think I've ever felt this good in my life. Maybe somewhere in my mind, a memory will surface where I was overwhelmed with emotion. Even if that were to happen, it wouldn't compare to this moment in time. What I've done for those women will be with them forever. I freed them from a lifetime of pain and possibly death. After all the stories I've heard of my past, I know in this life I have a heart. Hopefully, when I reunite with my mother, I will experience the same kind of love.

44 – KANE

We approached the room and before walking inside, I turned to the Snake and Bam. "I need to tell you something that might seem . . . crazy." They didn't say a word and kept their worried eyes on me. I could tell mentioning Abel brought some kind of joy in their lives which I sure as hell didn't understand. "Abel claims to have lost his memory in an accident."

". . .," Bam was lost for words. His eyes shifted on Snake as he searched for an answer.

"That's . . .," Snake eyes flickered between us. "Im . . . pos-sible."

I sighed. "If you say so. I find It hard to believe. Obviously, I think he's lying. Maybe you can jog his memory." I led the way and continued through the door. "Smoke!" I hurried over to him and dropped to my knees. He was sprawled out on the floor, lifeless. "Smoke," I called while propping my hand under his head. I looked around the room frantically, searching for Abel. "Fuck!"

"Is he dead?" Bear rushed over. "Fuck, man. I knew I should've stayed behind."

"Stop acting like pussies," I looked down at Smoke. His eyes were wide open and he had a smile on his face.

"Smoke," Bear said excitedly. "I thought you were gone, man."

"What happened to you," I asked.

"Stop staring into my eyes, nigga," He asked. "We're not in love."

I released his head and stood. It was the happiest I've felt in a while. My best friend was alive.

"Fuck," Smoke grabbed the back of his head. "I didn't say drop my shit." He slowly stood from the floor. "Damn, that shit hurt."

"My bad," I smiled, happy as hell I didn't lose him. "I didn't want you to feel like a hoe. Niggas solid, you feel me."

"Hell, nah, I don't feel you," he continued rubbing his head. "You should have given me a warning. One, two, three, release or some shit, my guy."

"Bruh," I looked at him sarcastically. "You said let go."

"Anyway," he sighed and picked his gun up from the floor. "I challenged Abel to a fight. I couldn't look at him after what happened to sis. I had to try'em. It was my fault he escaped. I thought he was about to kill me. Instead, he emptied the clip into the bed so I would shoot him in the back when he dipped."

"He kicked your ass," Bear spoke up. "Didn't he?"

"Please," Smoke sucked his teeth. "Nigga hit me once because I went for my strap."

258

"Damn," Bear awed. "One time, dawg. That's even worse. Dropped your ass."

"Man . . ., fuck you," Smoke told him. "He snuck me."

"So, he's gone," Snake asked.

"Fuck it look like," Smoke replied angrily. "Unless that nigga has an invisible spell."

"Did he mention anything before leaving," I asked.

"He went after Adrian," he answered. "I think he really intends to save Kim, real talk. He told you the truth about everything and he could have ended my shit. Dat nigga memory is gone. Either that or he found God. One hunnid."

"Maybe," I replied, taking it all in. There was no reason to be upset with Smoke. I couldn't blame him for what went down with Abel. Several things came to mind as I thought about the situation at hand. What would it look like if Abel and Adrian were working together? How would it benefit them? If Adrian wants to save Jordan. He would need to get the cure from Casanova. Abel came to Africa with the diamond, linked with our aunt, and went after my father's safe. Jordan is near death and the General captured Aayla. Hum, what am I missing? Abel gave up Jordan and went after Adrian. Adrian has Kim. "Fuck," I muttered, trying to get the puzzle pieces to fit.

"Yo," Bear said walking over to the window. "Did y'all hear that?"

"Yeah," Smoke spoke up. "Sounds like a fight."

"What is it," my thoughts were interrupted after Bear alerted us of something outside.

"Wow," Bear said looking out of the window. "We don't have to worry about where Aasir is anymore."

"Why," I said concerned. "Wassup?"

"Man," Bear began. "He's by the whips getting his ass kicked by four women."

"No bullshit," Smoke asked.

"Bruh," Bear backed away from the window. "If I'm lying, I'm dying."

Smoke hurried over and looked out of the window. "Hell, nah. Kane, get over here, man. You have to see this."

I moved Smoke out of the way and had a look for myself. Four women were giving Aasir the business. "What the fuck is goin' on?"

"Should we help," Bear asked. "I mean, damn. Shit doesn't seem fair."

"Hell, nah," Smoke said. "I'm not puttin' my hands on a woman."

"No, fool," Bear replied. "I'm talking about breaking up the fight. One of them looks like the woman who checked us in."

"She does look familiar," I said still observing the one-sided fight.

"Bruh must've been tryin' to get freaky deaky and didn't pay up," Smoke suggested. "You know how hoes be."

I backed away from the window. "Ight, look. This is what we're gonna do. Bear, take Snake and Bam back to the room with Big Bruce and Jordan. Pack everything. Don't forget to let Doo-Rag know. We need to get the fuck outta here after we get back Kim. Smoke and I will start looking for Adrian after we help Aasir. If Adrian is looking for me, all I have to do is be where he can find me. Adrian will release Kim for Jordan so I'll give you a call to bring him to the location. To sweetin' the deal, I'll throw in the diamond for insurance. He may not give a fuck about his brother and we might need another piece to negotiate. Are we clear?" I looked around the room.

"Fo' sho," Bear tossed me the African Black Diamond.

I caught the diamond and put it inside my pocket.

"Let's ride," Smoke replied.

"Alright then," I said and led the way out of the room.

Smoke and I hurried down the stairs and through the lobby. I heard one of the vehicles start as we pushed through the entrance. The four women who jumped Aasir pulled away in a hurry, leaving Aasir behind in a cloud of dust. He was sprawled out on the ground in the middle of the road.

I rushed over to Aasir and knelt beside him. "Are you good, dawg?" His chest was heaving so I knew he hadn't died. Fuck, I thought. This was all my fault. I had this man out here in a dangerous situation. Thankfully, it wasn't Adrian who got to him.

"I'm okay," he said as I helped him on his feet. He began dusting off his clothes.

261

"What happened," Smoke asked. "We saw you gettin' pieced the fuck up."

"I saw the women checking the vehicles," he answered. "I thought they were trying to sabotage us so I approached them. I told them to get away and they attacked me."

I looked around. "Well," I sighed. "They didn't take one of ours. That Jeep belonged to someone else."

"The bar," Aasir said before bending over and spitting up blood.

"Wha," I asked confused.

"The bar is closed and I saw two men go inside," he said while catching his breath. "One of them carried a woman inside."

"Kim," I said hysterically. "What did the men look like?"

"One wearing all-black," he groaned. "The other had a bald head."

"Fuckin' Abel," Smoke said. "I knew that nigga set us up."

"Thank you," I grabbed his shoulders and squeezed gently. "Tell the others to meet us at the bar and bring Jordan."

"You got it, sir," Aasir hurried inside the hotel.

"Let's fuck some shit up," Smoke pulled out his strap.

"No doubt," I did the same. "Fuckin' memory loss my ass."

45 – ABEL

I left the house and couldn't believe my eyes once I made it outside. I expected to see an enormous home. Instead, the home was an enormous two-story brick building that looked abandoned. You would've never expected the inside would be made into a beautiful home. Casanova didn't want anyone to find him or mess up his operation. This was actually a good strategy to stay off the radar. The building was located at the edge of town on the same road as the hotel and bar. I could see the hotel in the distance. No wonder there were no twists and turns when taking the underground passage to the basement of the home.

"Ok," I muttered. "Let's finish this." I took off in a sprint, heading toward the bar. It took me three minutes to reach the building. Roughly four minutes faster than the pathway underground. No one was out so I wasn't spotted. Kane and his crew were still inside the hotel when I passed by. I'm sure he found Smoke by now. It's been long enough. Hopefully, he'll see my true intentions.

I examined the front door of the bar, thinking about the bomb Adrian attached to our room door. Would he, I thought. I didn't want to risk opening the door and exploding into a million pieces. The man is an assassin, aiming to take out a group of men. He'll use every resource, tactic, and weapons to make things even. It wouldn't surprise me if the fucking building erupted and took down the block. I also had to be mindful of tripwires and other traps. I decided to find another entry point.

I strolled to the side of the building through the alley. I stopped where the rebel and I fought. I could've continued to the back of the building and tried the back door, but the risk was the same as using the front door. I stood there thinking about what happened less than a day ago. I killed a man. Even though I wasn't in the right state of mind, it was me. I wanted to feel sympathy for the man. However, the man who committed the crime emotions were detached from how I feel now. It was as if I wasn't there so how could I feel anything?

I stepped in front of the dumpster wondering if he was still inside. I sighed and looked up and spotted a window. Bingo, that was my way inside. I hopped on top of the dumpster. The window was chest level and large enough for me to fit through. I looked inside and scanned the area before checking if it was unlocked. It was early morning and yet it was dark on the inside. I couldn't see much. What am I doing here, I thought. A sense of regret came over me as I placed my fingertips on the window and slid it up. Look at that. The window was unlocked.

I poked my head through the window and looked down at the floor. It was about a twelve-foot drop. Nothing was in the way of entering the building into the kitchen area of the bar. I listened for Adrian or Kim to make a sound. It was completely silent. The only thing that could be heard was the humming sound coming from the generator. I began to worry if they were inside. Adrian could have switched it up a second time. No turning back now, I thought slipping through the window. I braced myself for the fall, trying to land as quietly as possible. I froze and listened for Adrian after hitting the floor. All good. I crept through the kitchen over to the bar doors. I wanted so badly to turn on the lights but I knew that would get me killed. Hell, it wouldn't make a difference if the lights were on or off. Adrian had the advantage.

I pushed through the doors out into the club area. The first thing that I noticed was the strobe lights over the dance floor were on and the song *"Kim"* by Eminem played through the speakers. Adrian had the chorus part of the song on repeat. It was a sarcastic way of saying, Kim was in the building and she wouldn't leave alive. I wasn't sure how I knew the song but I did. Maybe I'm a fan of his music.

I cautiously searched the area, hoping to spot Adrian before he caught me by surprise. This was a bad situation. I could feel death approaching. Not only was I terrified of what he would do to me. I kept the gun holstered in my waistband. Adrian could easily misinterpret my intentions if I had it out. Damn, I had to get it under control. I felt sweat stream off my forehead down to the tip of my nose. Time slowed as it rolled off my nose to the floor in slow motion and disintegrated.

I looked up from the ground after rejoining reality. Stairs. There was a roped-off section that led to the second floor of the establishment. I hurried over, unhooked the rope, and looked toward the top of the section. I slowly made my way up, continuously keeping an eye over my shoulder. I saw two doors directly across from each other after reaching the top of the stairs. The door on the right had a gold VIP plate and the door on the left had nothing on it. I stood between the rooms trying to decide which one to enter first.

I stepped in front of the door that read VIP and inspected the frame for traps. I put my hand on the knob and turned. Perfect, I thought. He wants me to come inside. There was no sense in creeping through when it was surely being monitored by Adrian. He wouldn't make a mistake by not having eyes on it.

Instead of looking suspicious, I just opened the door and called his name. "Adrian." I stood there shocked, yet to cross the threshold. My eyes grew wide, stunned by who I saw. Not because Adrian was nowhere to be found. Kim was gagged and tied to the bed. She didn't shout my name this time because her head was down. She appeared to be unaware of her surroundings and possibly unconscious. Adrian might have knocked her out to keep her quiet. That assumption didn't explain why he would leave the door unlocked. Before I had time to

266

think about my next move, my mouth was covered and I was pulled back forcefully. I had no doubt the person who snatched me was Adrian.

"You called," Adrian's voice terrified me. It was the sound of a killer after catching his prey.

". . .," I couldn't speak with Adrian's hand covering my mouth. What would I say anyway? My initial thought was to try to reason with him. Adrian was swift and quiet. I never had a chance. He knew my position the whole time. At the very least, he knew when I reached the second level. He could have easily slit my throat.

Adrian slammed my head against the wall which tripled the pain from previous fights with Kane and Smoke. I tried to backpaddle him into the wall. He was either too strong or he wore spiked cleats. He didn't budge. Imagine leaning back into a building and trying to move it. That's what it felt like.

I finally got the chance to see what was behind door number two. However, it wasn't how I intended. The door with no plate was filled with security equipment. I crashed into several monitors before falling to the floor. Well, I was right about Adrian clocking my position. "Adrian," I held up my hand. My heart was beating fast enough to explode. I took a deep breath just to get the next few words out of my mouth. "Let me explain."

Adrian stepped through the door with a smile on his face. "I don't need an explanation. I know what you did. You should've stayed put like I asked and just . . . maybe after all this was over. I would've let you walk out of here alive. Instead, you led Kane to my brother. The only reason Jordan kept you alive was to find Kane. You should have left, Abel. Look at the bright side, I never give my victims an explanation."

"Wait," I couldn't give up after what he said. There was still a chance. I shook off the dizziness while struggling to stand on my feet.

"No, I can't," Adrian spun a dagger on his palm as he approached. "I have to kill you before Kane arrives."

"I have the –" Adrian lunged at me before I had a chance to inform him of the cure. I wanted to exchange it for Kim. He could save Jordan and Kane would possibly trust me again. It was worth the risk of saving my family.

I caught Adrian's arm as he tried to stab my chest. He pushed forward and I moved backwards a foot or two. He was incredibly stronger than I expected. We struggled for over thirty seconds trying to get the upper hand. Somehow, I had to outmuscle him. The tip of the dagger began to poke through my skin directly over the liver. Another inch and Adrian would successfully end my life. The attack would be fatal due to the reservatory blood in the organ.

"I can save . . . Jordan," I grunted while slightly overpowering him.

Adrian smirked as if it was a light day at work. He didn't appear to struggle nearly as much. His cold stare had one goal in mind and that was to kill me. Nothing else mattered to him. He was enjoying every second of our fight.

Fuck, I thought. He's even crazier than his brother. Before I knew what hit me, Adrian used my weight against me. He fell back, stuck his foot in my stomach as I came down on him, and flipped me through the door into the hall. The fall wasn't bad and I was able to quickly get on my feet. It didn't help that Adrian had grabbed the top frame of the door and kicked me in the chest. The force behind the kick sent me back into the door of the VIP room. "Ah," my spine connected with the edge of the frame. I clenched my teeth and scutched my face, trying to absorb the pain. While in the moment of agony, Adrian side-kicked the right side of my head and I stumbled toward the stairs. I felt another kick in my back and dropped to my knees. Everything happened fast. I was unable to recover in time for the next move. Adrian's attacks were at Godspeed.

I wanted to run for my life but I couldn't find it in my heart to abandon Kim. How can I defeat this monster, I thought. He trained to assassinate people. There was nothing he wouldn't do to win. This was a game to him. I should've been dead. I felt Adrian closing in as I sat on my knees. The gun was still under my shirt, tucked in my waistband. I doubted if I was fast enough to pull it out and aim at Adrian without him disarming me. I had to decide. Adrian was on my neck.

Suddenly, Adrian flipped over my head and was now in front of me. He grabbed the sides of my skull with his hands. Shit, I thought. He was ready to break my neck. I quickly reached for the gun. The safety was off and I chambered a bullet earlier. I just had to aim and pull the trigger. The barrel of the gun pressed against his gut. I saw the expression on his face change and his eyes instantly grew wide as I pulled back the trigger.

"Fuck," he realized he was about to die. He released my head and swiftly moved to the side.

I knew I caught him when his body jerked and he fell against the wall to the floor. We both were at the end but I had the advantage. He began to stand as did I. I aimed the weapon ready to finish off Adrian. "Wha," the top barrel of the gun was gone. I held the lower receiver in shock unable to fire.

"Missing something," Adrian held up the barrel and tossed it down the hall. He kept his right hand over the wound so he wouldn't bleed out. He leaned against the wall to prevent falling back to the floor.

I couldn't believe he was fast enough to remove the pin from the weapon and detach the barrel. He's hurt. That was the only thing that came to mind. Assassin or not, the man took a bullet. His strength, speed, and agility couldn't be the same. The playing field was even. I acted by rushing at Adrian. He wasn't fast enough to dodge me. The first blow went to his stomach. I aimed where he was shot. He tried his best to shield the wound from getting hit. I kept at it as if I were a maniac. Over and over again. I threw numerous shots to his stomach and head area. Adrian was slow and becoming more defenseless as time passed.

"Ah," Adrian groaned while struggling to stop my assault. "You can't save him."

I didn't respond. There was nothing for me to say. Adrian wanted me to know that he would do everything in his power to annihilate my brother. What he didn't know was I would do anything to save him.

I wrapped Adrian in a bear hug and squeezed with all of my might. His arms were locked inside the hold preventing him from striking with his fists. We fell wall to wall toward the stairs. I maintained my balance and grip. Adrian's eyes began to fade and I felt his tense body weaken. He was on the verge of passing out. A few more seconds and it would be done. Suddenly, his head fell back as if he were dead, and in an instant, Adrian's head came full force, and blasted me in the skull. "Ah," I released the hold and dropped Adrian after the headbutt. Every active nerve in my body felt as though they were in my forehead. My body was pulled downward without a second to recover.

"Ah," Adrian shouted in my ear as we tumbled down the stairs.

". . .," every step I crashed into caused excruciating pain. I have never been more grateful than when it was over. My entire body ached to the core. I couldn't tell where Adrian landed because I kept my eyes shut, thinking it would ease the fall. I lay sprawled out at the bottom of the steps for what seemed like an eternity. I took a deep breath and exhaled exhaustedly.

". . .," I heard him but had yet to set my eyes on him.

The only thing worse than the pain I felt had to be death. Get up, I told myself. I opened my eyes and watched the ceiling for several seconds contemplating my decisions. Come on. Get up before he kills you. I couldn't. My legs wouldn't allow me to stand. My arms wouldn't move and my neck stiffened. I felt broken for the time being. ". . .," I groaned trying to move. Adrian could get up before me and my time on earth would be for nothing or I could overcome the pain and be a hero. "Fuck," I tried forcing my arms to move. It was looking like the first option where Adrian would prevail. One more go, I thought. Soon, Adrian would be on his feet, dagger to my neck, and a quick slice across my throat. The thought was horrifying to mull over.

Finally, I was able to sit up. Adrian landed hard enough to knock himself out. He lay serval feet from the steps. The fall wasn't as generous to him. Unfortunately, I knew he wasn't dead so time was of the essence. I thought about wrapping my hands around his neck or even placing my boat over it, but my last bit of strength had to be used for one purpose.

I got on my feet and made my way to the VIP room. Kim remained in the same position as before the attack. I stumbled over and undid the binds. She fell free into my arms. "Kim," I tried to wake her by tapping the side of her cheek. She didn't come around after several attempts. "Kim," she was unresponsive. I removed her from the bed and carried her out of the room. The hall was clear. I stumbled off-balanced toward the stairs. Nearly dropped her on two occasions because my arms were weak, and my legs drained of energy. I put my back against the wall to prevent falling another time as I made my way down the stairs.

No, I thought. Adrian wasn't where I left him. I scanned the area frantically for the assassin. I should've put the gun back together. It was too late for that with Kim in my arms. I pushed forward toward the door and kicked through. I saw several individuals as I crossed the threshold. One of them was my mother.

46 – KANE

Smoke and I made it in front of the bar in no time. I tried opening the door. "Fuck," I said frustrated. "It's locked." I sighed and looked at Smoke.

Smoke cupped his hands and looked through the small window on the door. "Shid, it sounds like it's going down in there. I hear music." Smoke backed away from the door. "Crazy mufucka playin' Eminem. We have to hurry. They could be doing something to sis."

"Let's try the back door," I said. "Unless you have another idea?"

Smoke shook his head, "I'm fresh out of ideas. Back door."

Right when we turned to head around the building. Three Jeeps with Libya flag decals on the sides pulled up to a harsh stop. We froze in our tracks. Damn, this ain't good, I thought and eyed Smoke from the corner of my eyes. I saw the same expression on his face. The shit was about to hit the fan.

"What the fuck," Smoke muttered. "You wanna run for it? I got this shit."

"Nah," I said, thinking about what would happen to him. "I can't leave you."

"What about sis," he replied, keeping his eyes locked on the vehicles.

"One thing at a time," I said. "Besides, I have what they want."

"The diamond," Smoke asked. "I fuckin' love you, bruh."

"Let's make this quick," I said, watching the doors open on each of the vehicles. What I saw next was breathtaking. My mother emerged from the middle vehicle with the girl who attempted to kill Kim. Two soldiers stepped out of the vehicle as well. Ten Libyan soldiers surrounded Gina and my mother. What the fuck is going on, I thought as my mother stepped forward. The soldiers fell in line as if they were waiting for her orders.

"My beautiful boy," my mother stopped after taking a few steps in my direction. I estimated at least fifteen yards between us. "How have you been?"

"I'm good, mother," I said skeptically. "What are you doing here and with them?" I took a step in her direction and the soldiers quickly drew their weapons. I held up my hands.

My mother held up her hand and the soldiers fell back in line.

I looked back at Smoke and he was ready. "Smoke," I watched him lower his weapon. I turned my attention back to my mother.

"Somethin' ain't right, bruh," I heard Smoke over my shoulder. "What's up with mom? She with these niggas?"

"You wouldn't understand why I'm here," my mother said. "You need to leave this place immediately. Take your friends and go home."

"What do you mean I wouldn't understand," I asked, keeping my eyes on her. It was as if no one else was there but us. "Why don't you just tell me, mother? You were with Jordan and now you're with the General's army. I saw what was in father's black notebook. He wasn't a banker. He was a weapons smuggler. I know why you lied to us when we were young. You were trying to protect us from this life. My father is gone and it's up to me to protect you from this life. So, if you want me to go home, you come with me. I won't leave here without you." I held out my hand to her.

"You are your father," my mother told me. "Unfortunately, I cannot leave. You're father and I made a promise to one another that we would finish what we started when we left Jamaica years ago."

"And you think you can fulfill that promise with Jordan and the General and not your son," I asked frustrated. "I don't know who you are anymore. You and your secrets. I know about my aunt. You hid her from me. That's right. I saw a fuckin' picture of her and my father on a wall in Mizdah."

"You watch your mouth when you're speakin' to me," my mother said angrily and pointed your finger at me. I don't think I've ever seen her instantly get this mad at me. "I'm still your mother."

"Are you," I said with tears in my eyes. I didn't plan to be this emotional at this time. Kim needed me and I'm here arguing with my mother over family issues.

"My son, I –"

"Just stop," I said and looked to the side. I couldn't face my mother. Looking at her was hard on my soul. She's hurt me time and time again and I couldn't take her lying straight to my face. "You don't have to say anything else to me. I have what you want. I realize this is the only thing that matters to you." I retrieved the diamond from my pocket and held it up for everyone to see.

". . .," my mother was speechless.

"The diamond," I heard Gina mutter while gawking at it.

"You can have it," I said while cautiously walking in her direction. "Do what you need to do with it. I don't care anymore." I understood time was running short. The only person I needed to save was the love of my life.

My mother walked toward me and suddenly, the door to the bar burst open.

I turned toward the commotion and so did everyone else, guns ready. "Kim!"

"Not you, not you," Kim shouted in Abel's arms as he ran from the bar. "I hate you!"

I put the diamond in my mother's hands and ran toward Abel. Kim whaled on Abel's face and he stumbled to the ground. Kim fell from

277

his arms and rolled a foot forward. She went at Abel while he was down and continued beating on him.

"I hate you," she shouted. "I hate you!"

I grabbed Kim from behind and pulled her away from Abel. She struggled to get free, kicking and throwing punches as I restrained her. "It's me, baby. It's Kane."

"Keep your fuckin' hands off of my man," I heard Gina from behind.

"I'll blow off your fuckin' head," I heard Smoke. "Put the gun away bitch."

Kim and I stumbled to the ground. She fell between my legs. We were in a sitting position. "It's me, baby. Calm down. You're safe."

"I hate you," She shouted one last time at Abel and began to cry.

"It's ok," I held Kim close as if I would never see her again. "I won't let him hurt you." I kissed her on the cheek, trying to calm her down. Nothing else mattered in the world but her. Not Abel, Jordan, Adrian, the diamond, or my mother. The only thing on my mind was leaving Africa alive with my true family. The ones who put their lives on the line for me. The ones who have been there through thick and thin. My crew.

"Look at what we have here," I looked toward the voice.

"Adrian," he was casually sitting on the edge of the bar's rooftop.

"It's me," he said sarcastically. "Great show by the way. I wanted to intervene earlier but it was too juicy. I mean . . . the whole ordeal with your mother and then the scene with Abel. Man, you guys should have your own TV show."

"You want me to smack this fuck boy," Smoke asked, taking his attention off Gina.

"We have Kim," I told him. "Fuck'em. Let's get out of here."

"Do you," Adrian held up a device. "You might want to reconsider." He pointed at Kim.

Fuck, I thought. I noticed Kim had something strapped around her ankle. "What the fuck did you strapped to her leg?" I stood and helped Kim stand. She kept her arms around me and continued to sob in my chest.

"That my friend is enough dynamite to level the entire block," Adrian said. "I click this button and kaboom! I'll see you, you, you, you, and all of you in hell. You might be the only one that gets into Heaven."

Adrian pointed at me, Smoke, Gina, my mother, and all of the soldiers. Kim was the only person he thought would make it into Heaven. At least he was being honest. "We'll hand over Jordan if you take off the dynamite."

"Speaking of my brother," Adrian looked at the watch on his wrist. "He should be here any . . . minute now."

Suddenly, Aasir's taxi came speeding down the road and slid to a stop.

"Right on time," Adrian said.

"Aasir," I said as he hopped out of the vehicle. "What are you doing here? You should be with the others."

"It's him," Adrian stood on his feet.

"It's who," I asked. I watched Abel point at Aasir.

"Casanavo," Abel appeared to be exhausted.

I shook my head unable to grasp the idea of Aasir kidnapping Kim. "There's no way he's Cas —"

"It's him, baby," Kim whispered in my ear. "Aasir is Casanova."

"Did you do what I asked," Adrian looked at Aasir.

"Your brother is in the van," Aasir told him.

"Why would you do this to us," I asked Aasir.

Aasir smiled. "I was never on your side. I kidnap women for a living."

"You dirty mufucka," Smoke said.

"I spotted her at the airport," Aasir continued. "I would have had her if she wasn't with a group of men. I took you where you needed to go until I found the best time to separate her from the group. You were paying good money for travel. I couldn't resist. She was worth the wait and just so you know, I won't sell this one on the market. She will be my wife."

"You must be out of your fuckin' mind if you think I'll let that happen," I growled.

"Gentlemen," Adrian held up his hands. "Unfortunately, I must depart."

280

"What about the woman," Aasir asked.

"Nigga," Smoke looked at Aasir. "I'll put one in you right now if you touch her."

"Hand over the girl," Adrian held up the device. "Or we all die."

"I rather die," I said seriously.

"Your call," Adrian replied.

"Wait," Abel held up something to Adrian. "You want the cure, right? That's what all of this is about. This is it. I'll give it to you for the detonator."

Abel had a small tube with a green substance in it. He has the cure, I thought.

"Now that's a good offer," Adrian catted down the side of the building and was on the ground in an instant. He kept his finger on the detonator as he approached Abel. "How do I know it's the real thing."

"You can't do this to me," Aasir shouted. "We have a deal!"

"The woman at the mansion confirmed it," Abel told him. "They knew exactly what it was when I showed it to them."

"You can't –" Aasir was interrupted. A dragger appeared in his throat. Blood began to gush freely and rapidly. Aasir pulled the dagger from his neck and fell to his knees. I watched his eyes roll to the back of his head as he fell forward to the ground dead.

"Your services are no longer needed," Adrian said with his arm out toward Aasir. He sighed and focused on Abel. "If my brother dies from this. I kill you ten times over."

281

"I'm fine with that," Abel told him.

"Ok," Adrian said. "Walk with me to the van. Once I'm in the vehicle we can make the trade."

I kept Kim in my arms as Adrian and Abel walked by. I couldn't believe what Abel was doing for Kim or maybe, he was doing it to save his own ass. The bomb was powerful enough to kill us all. Why wouldn't he make the deal?

Adrian checked the van, making sure Jordan was inside before he got in the driver's seat. Abel stepped to the door and made the exchange. Dust from the van's tires filled the air as Adrian vanished in the distance.

All eyes were on Abel as he stood there with the detonator. "The deal won't stop them from killing us." Abel took his eyes on the device. "We have to work together to stop them. Once Jordan is well. They will come."

"Let's drive away, baby," Gina spoke up. "We have the detonator and the diamond."

"I can't do that," Abel looked at her. "I don't know who you are and they're my family."

"I'm the love of your life," Gina stepped forward. "We'll do anything for each other."

"I'm sorry," Abel told her. "I don't remember who you are."

"Is this some kind of game you're playing," Gina erupted. "You'll save that bitch but forget about me. The one who's been there for you. I'll die for you, Abel."

". . .," Abel sighed. "I'm sorry about how you feel. I have to protect my family. It's the only way to redeem what I've done in the past." He turned his attention away from Gina. "Kane, this is for you." He held out the device.

I released Kim and walked over to Abel. Something caught his attention because his eyes grew wide as fuck.

"No," Abel shouted and bolted past me.

Boom!

Abel was on top of Kim, lying on the ground. I ran over to them as gunfire erupted.

"Fuck," Smoke returned fire.

I fell to my knees. Not giving a fuck if I got hit. I had to reach Kim. I crawled on my hands and knees the rest of the way. I spotted a pool of blood next to them. Neither of them moved. I couldn't tell who was hit or if they were dead.

"We gotta get the fuck outta here, bruh," I heard Smoke shout.

Bullets whizzed by my head as I pried Abel from Kim. He fell off to the side.

"I'm ok," Kim told me. "I wasn't hit."

"Thank God," I looked and Abel, and he didn't move. "Abel," I called and Smoke began to tug on my shoulder, shouting at me to get up. "Abel," I shook him. He's gone, I thought. He sacrificed his life to save Kim. I didn't know how to feel. Everything we've been through together surfaced. I dreamed of killing him for what he'd done to our family. I never imagined it would hurt this bad now that he's dead. I looked back at my mother. She hurried to the Jeep and got inside with Gina. I saw the look in her eyes before they pulled away. She didn't shed a tear. Abel was dead to her after killing her husband. She wasn't aware of his memory loss. Would she have cared if it were true? I looked back at Abel. I couldn't leave him behind. He was my brother. The man who put his life on the line for our family. There was one thing my father told me to never forget. Blood is thicker than water. "Abel . . .!"

Author Bio

King Coopa J was born December 24, 1983, in Indianapolis, Indiana. He began writing fiction while incarcerated in 2010. Reading street literature inspired him to become a writer. He also has a passion for reading mystery, thriller & suspense novels. Kane, his first book, was created after making a bet with an inmate that he could write a novel. He currently lives in Maryland with his two sons.

Made in the USA
Monee, IL
08 October 2024

67369570R00173